All Shorts

CW00802590

by the

Ten Green Jotters

Dear Chris and Caitlin

Enjoy.

Love
Richard

PublishNation
www.publishnation.co.uk

CONTENTS

FOREWORD

Following on from the success of their first collection of tales, *Literary AllShorts*, the Ten Green Jotters turned their minds to that most challenging of genres: Crime. And a challenge it turned out to be!

Written in the depths of the Covid pandemic, when literary endeavour was perhaps the last thing on their minds, inspiration was hard fought for. Nevertheless, it was not found wanting in aiming to please readers who deserve some respite and entertainment during these tough times.

So, if you like your detectives hardboiled, tables being turned, and revenge as a dish served cold, you will find this and more in these pages; a crime to suit every palate. All sorts, in fact, in *All Shorts of Crime*.

THE OTHER ROOM

By Jan Brown

Torch glare shielded, he cautiously eased the back door open and stood in the darkened hallway, listening intently for signs of life. He'd been watching this property for a few weeks now and was pretty confident the elderly couple weren't in the habit of entertaining overnight guests. As far as he could tell from his observations, they had very few visitors; the postman seemed to be the only person who occasionally came to the front door. The house looked pukka, though.

Mikey was still smarting from the last ear bashing he'd received from Sonia: '*You've never got any money, you never take me anywhere, you don't love me, blah blah.*' He'd tried to tell her it wasn't that easy. Once you'd put money aside for the essentials – beer and fags, and a drop of blow – there wasn't that much left. Anyway, the result of that was Sonia had actually thrown him out of the flat, his own home. Well, strictly speaking it wasn't his home or hers; it belonged to some geezer who'd spent the last few months trying to get them evicted. They'd prevented this by good team working, one of them always staying in the property, but all of a sudden that wasn't enough for Sonia; she wanted to be taken out to restaurants and the cinema. What was wrong with a burger and chips and what-have-you on the sofa? He didn't get birds; whatever you did, it wasn't right.

He became aware of a low rumbling coming from upstairs and, Sonia woes forgotten, he grinned to himself. Great, snoring. Whoever it was hadn't heard a thing, so no need to get nasty. He didn't want to hurt anyone, but everyone has to make a living. Mikey opened one of the large holdalls he'd brought with him and, lifting a heavy brown clock from the mantelpiece, he placed it into the bag. He added some frames that looked like silver, not bothering to remove the personal photos, and then headed for the kitchen. They'd probably have quality cutlery, and maybe a money tin. He knew old people often hid their money in tins.

'Hello, what you up to?'

Mikey stopped still; in fact, he almost stopped breathing. Someone was already in the kitchen. How did they get down the stairs without him hearing? Or maybe they'd already been there, creeping about. Whatever, he'd not been caught for a few years and his legs went to jelly. He couldn't do time again. Sonia definitely wasn't the waiting type.

'Alright?'

His heart thumping, Mikey peered into the kitchen and, not immediately seeing anyone, rapidly swung the torch beam around the whole room. It focused on a massive bird cage that took up most of the back area. The happy chattering continued from under the cover thrown over the cage.

'You're lovely, you are. Hello, what you up to?'

Mikey whipped off the cover and stared at the grey and green bird, who seemed to stare back at him with black, beady eyes. He wasn't actually in a cage; it was more like an open plan living area, complete with food and water tubs and lots of hanging toys.

'Hello,' Mikey responded. 'You'll be worth a bit of money, I think. Got to catch you first though.'

The bird (Mikey figured it was a parrot) turned its head almost upside down and stared at him. 'Alright? What's your name? My name's Rocky.'

Mikey rubbed his hands together. 'Pleased to meet you, Rocky. You're a big bugger, ain't you? Certainly ain't no budgie.' He knew this as he had once been given a budgie as a small child, but hadn't been allowed to keep it when he'd changed foster families.

Grabbing a tea towel, Mikey advanced towards the bird, which promptly took flight and settled itself on top of a wall unit out of Mikey's reach. 'You bloody bugger!' he cursed. 'But I can wait.'

Mikey added to his holdall rabbit-shaped salt and pepper pots, another clock and a blue and white vase before opening another cupboard. 'Oh yes!' he whispered, spotting the gleaming silver knives, forks and spoons displayed in their blue velvet case. 'Come on, this is what I'm talking about.'

Rocky had returned to his perch and, occupied by food, failed to notice Mikey advancing until it was too late. Mikey grabbed at him and held him tightly in his hands, preventing him flying off or even turning his head.

'Ha, I've got you now, you little sod. Not so clever now, are you?' Triumphantly, Mikey raised up his trophy towards the ceiling. 'Like Viera winning the FA Cup for Arsenal, this is. Bloody pukka.' Inspired by his victory, Mikey held his prize towards his face as if to kiss it.

Rocky wasn't having any of that and took the chance to bite viciously into Mikey's nose, hanging on for painful seconds even after Mikey had inevitably released him.

'Argh, you bit me! I'll strangle you for that when I get hold of you.' He cupped his throbbing nose and stared at the blood dripping through his fingers and spotting onto the floor.

Rocky had flown back up to the top of the unit, the feathers on top of his head huge and ruffled. Switching on the kitchen light and pocketing his torch, Mikey began angrily throwing objects up at the bird, who dodged them with ease as he stared down at his attacker with dark, lively eyes. 'Hello, hello, hello,' he squawked, nodding his head in time, increasing the clamour in the already noisy kitchen.

'What are you doing in my house?'

Lots of little hairs on the back of Mikey's neck immediately stood up. 'That's not the bird speaking, is it?' he asked, miserably.

'No, indeed it is not. Turn around, young man.'

Mikey shuffled rather than turned around. Facing him was an old man with neat, white hair and tartan slippers, a shotgun pointing steadily at him.

'Don't shoot me... I'm sorry.'

'You're sorry for what? Breaking in, attacking Rocky, ruining the kitchen or getting caught?'

'Well, all of it, obviously. I don't want any trouble. Are you going to call the pigs?'

'Well, first of all I rather think I want to communicate with my wife and make sure poor Rocky is okay. In the meantime, you had better wait in the other room.'

The old man directed Mikey through another door, slamming it shut behind him. Mikey looked around the gloomy room that he found himself in. He could see a few impressive bowls, a lot of dead house plants and a nice fluffy green rug. He bent down to inspect it closely and, from that position, registered the rocking chair sitting upon it… and the splayed-out legs wearing the shiny black shoes. A figure with hollow eyes and a macabre grin occupied the rocking chair.

'Whoa… God!' Mikey leapt up and raced for the door; it would not open. 'Hey, let me out. Help, help!'

'You might as well be quiet.' The old man's voice emerged from a small wireless box on the table and boomed around the room. 'It's all soundproofed and airtight so there's no point in making a fuss.'

'What is this? I thought you were going to talk to your wife? You've left me in here with a body.'

'Yes, he was one of those scammer people; you know, trying to trick me. I always think he looks rather comfortable in the rocking chair. What do you think about those two on the sofa? Quite romantic in a banal sort of way.'

Stiff with dread, Mikey forced his eyes towards the velvet green sofa and the young couple dressed in matching jeans and t-shirts, their arms covered in tattoos and their faces frozen in rictus grimaces that he only associated with horror films. The boy's right middle finger was raised in a final rebellious contortion.

'Of course, they thought they were the clever ones, breaking their way in – rather like you, I imagine.' The old man chuckled grotesquely. 'Anyway, it is good of you to join us, but I must get the show on the road, young man.'

Mikey looked around in confusion. He could hear a noise, a sort of hissing, and he began to pull desperately at the door again. 'Let me out! You're not gassing me. Help me!'

'Oh no, dear boy, that's not my intention at all. No, that would be dangerous. What I'm doing is removing the oxygen from the room; a cleaner death, if you like. I am quite environmentally aware, you know.'

'Don't do this, please. What about your wife? Did you talk to her?'

'I didn't say *talk*,' the man said mildly, 'I said *communicate*. No, I couldn't get through to her. If you look very carefully in the far corner of the room, you will see that she is quite, quite dead. She wanted to leave, you see, and I couldn't let her. Of course, in a few moments you might be able to connect with her on a higher plane than I.'

Mikey slipped to the floor and, for no reason at all, his last thought was of a grey and green parrot. It looked at him with its dark, lively eyes.

'Alright?' it said.

A BUSINESS OF CHANCE

By C.G. Harris

I know nervous when I see it.

I'd never met this Dooley, but I could tell he was the one sitting with his back to the wall and his eyes to the door. He was nursing a whiskey when I walked into the Elm Bar; it was a Jameson's, and a large one at that, but it didn't seem to be cheering him. I'll say right now that, he being a stool pigeon, I can understand why; if certain guys become wise to how he makes a few extra bucks his wife, if he has one, may notice that he doesn't come home one night – or any other. I have a kind of sneaking admiration for these guys, if not the dirty work itself. For that reason, I would never call him Stoolie Dooley, like Jastrow from the 14th precinct did when he rang me. I'd been told his name was Patrick but I wouldn't call him that either, or Paddy or Pat – Dooley was good enough. In the P.I business if you call someone by their first name you've got way too close.

I don't have a usual watering hole, unless you count my apartment on La Salle, but if I did, I could do worse than the Elm Bar in the Village. It's out of my way but it's small and clean and just busy enough in the day not to get noticed, and it's dark in the corners if you want a little discreet conversation. The downside being, I heard, that they played folk music in the evenings and poets and writers conversed here. Art and politics ain't my thing; a little jazz and chess is enough after an empty day at the office, which is often. When it's a busy one I'm usually footing it around town after husbands or wives who are never together; it's the sort of work I've got comfortable with. I didn't want that to change, but it seemed to me just lately there were too many jobs falling my way of the type not good for my health: blackmail, corruption, homicides, to name a few. Those are things for the cops. I had a feeling this meeting with Dooley would throw up something I didn't like, but a favour for Jastrow would be returned, I knew, and he was the nearest thing to a buddy I was likely to get.

I removed my hat, rapped it to clear off the snow and ordered a small beer, not cold. Outside, January was doing its thing and New Yorkers were slipping and sliding their way through the late afternoon. I took my beer to the corner where the nervous guy sat, his head just above the pages of the Brooklyn Eagle that he wasn't reading. Unbuttoning my coat, I sat down opposite him while he folded the paper over neater than I would have given him credit for and placed it on the table. Up close he was younger than I thought he'd be – a couple of years less than me, I guessed thirty-one or two – but not fresh faced; he was worn around the eyes and there was a shrapnel scar on his neck. He wasn't quite as scared as I thought, either. Yeah, he played with his glass and stroked the side of his mouth from time to time, and those dark eyes were pretty quick at moving from side to side, but when they looked at me, they were straight and firm.

"Mr. Baum, is it?" He rose a little in my estimation when he said that; it was the 'mister' that did it. The slight Irish accent made it easier too.

I just about returned the favour, though it wasn't easy, thinking about the sort of company he might keep. "I wouldn't be here if I wasn't, Mr. Dooley." I nodded at the newspaper. "A little way from home, aren't you?"

"A trip across the river is good for me in this case, Mr. Baum. Healthier for me than a day out to Coney Island."

"Uh huh. So, what have you got? I'm in a hurry. I have a cat who needs feeding."

"Do you gamble?"

"Every day, Mr. Dooley. On whether I'm going to get hustled, beaten up or just not get paid…but no, you can't gamble in this state."

He managed a laugh. "It depends who you know, Mr. Baum. But of course, you know that already."

"So?"

He turned serious and leaned forward. "Someone is going to get hurt real bad, or worse…"

I nodded. "It's a chancy business. Anyone in particular?"

It was then that Dooley noticed the bar was filling up. To me, it looked like the usual Manhattan crowd was looking for a reason not to go home, but it seemed to spook him and he

11

suddenly stood and put his hat on. This meeting was going to be a lot shorter than I thought – and not so sweet.

"You don't have a wife by any chance, do you?" I said.

He stared at me like I was crazy and ignored my question. But he looked a little startled and, somehow, I figured he did.

"You should read the papers a little more, Mr. Baum." He slid the Eagle towards me. "Page three," he whispered.

"Is that it? Listen, bud," I said, reaching for the twenty bucks in my pants pocket, "I was told to give you this. But you ain't told me anything. I'm not sure you've earned it."

He looked angry, but I wasn't sure why until he sneered and said: "You cops are all the same. Selling or buying, money is the answer, ain't that right? Read it."

"Hey, I ain't a co-" But he was gone, head down and pushing his way through the growing crowd.

I was left feeling kind of aggrieved at his attitude. I ain't ever seen a stoolie refuse money before and for some reason it left me feeling dirty. Something about it didn't feel right.

I scowled and pulled the paper open at page three. The by-line hit me straightaway: *'Brooklyn Graft? Corruption, City and the Cops'*. There was a red circle around the reporter, one Ted Byrnes – and a black cross through his name.

I figured I'd better get back to Jastrow straight away.

*

I like my own company, but I ain't unsocial. I like to surprise the occasional visitor to my apartment with how tidy I can make it; I'm a bachelor but not a bum. Jastrow had seen it before: my high-back chair; the beat-up couch for visitors, a slender two-seater; the coffee table with the chess set on it. It was a good set, carved and worn. When he arrived and I'd given him a bourbon he couldn't help but pick up one of the pieces; no one ever can. Outside, the evening had drawn in, the snow had picked up again, and Manhattanville was getting ready to hunker down for the night. I closed the blinds and the glow from the table lamp made me and Jastrow and the cat look agreeable and domesticated.

I threw Jastrow a question. "What do you know about Dooley?"

"Me? Nothing."

"Nothing? You called him Stoolie. Ain't you on intimate terms?"

"Never met him. Never heard of him before today. I was told he was a pigeon with something to say and with a name like Dooley what else would I call him?"

I sighed. "Start again. Who told you, and why'd you ask me to see him?"

He put down his glass and stroked the cat. "It ain't so usual, I'll give you that. You remember Egan?"

"We all spent time at Iwo Jima, didn't we? You don't forget that. Yes, I remember him."

"Well, he rings me up yesterday, see? Says this guy called his precinct and wants to speak to someone, urgent – but not anyone there at Brooklyn. Egan's a sergeant there now..."

"Sergeant?" I scowled, thinking of my own pay check, which comes along in cash as and when.

"Bummer ain't it?" laughed Jastrow. "Anyway, the guy won't give his name or spill what it's about so Egan tells him he ain't got time for pussyfooting – no name, nothin' doing. Finally, he tells him it's Dooley and Egan gives him someone to speak to – that was me."

"So...what does Egan think?"

Jastrow shrugged. "He figured he's just some low life spilling the beans on some scam. Possibly a runner for one of the bookmakers, so he might have something worth saying."

I sat up. "Bookmakers? Like, say, Grossman? Oscar Grossman?"

"Well, sure, Grossman is one as it happens..."

I threw the Eagle across to him. I'd read the article through three times and I rolled a chess piece between my fingers as Jastrow read it himself. When he finished, he drained his glass. "This why you invited me over tonight?" he asked.

"I felt more comfortable away from the station after reading it. And Dooley refused my money, so that's bothering me. What's his pitch...? What are you thinking?"

Jastrow rubbed his chin for a while. Finally, he said: "Listen, so some reporter, this..." he looked at the paper "...this Byrnes, he's got some beef about Grossman running a couple of illegal wire room shops and making books on the gee-gees. He wants a story. He's there to sell papers, ain't he?"

I laughed. "You don't believe that, buddy. It's more than just a few crooked wire-rooms. Grossman is moving into the big time. And it's more than the horses – there are prize-fights, the big games…but that ain't the point, is it?" I leaned forward. "Here's the real story. He says there's graft…the cops are taking bribes to turn a blind eye."

Jastrow shrugged. "It's been known, sure, but low-level stuff."

I shook my head and poured myself a larger whisky. "Grossman is a heavy-pocketed fixer. If Byrnes is right, it ain't just the precincts, it could go up to division…and higher."

"So, what am I suppo-"

I put up my hand. "I'll be honest. I don't like crooks. And I don't like crooked cops. I couldn't be a cop myself, I tried it…but you're all needed. *They* need you," I flicked my head towards the window, "and they need you honest. But right now, I'm more worried about *this*." I stabbed my finger down on the paper and held it there under Ted Byrnes' name. The name with a black cross through it. "We've been given the head's up, Jastrow. By someone who doesn't take money for spilling the beans."

"Well?"

"Jastrow, they're going to kill him and all we've got to say so is a cross through his name – but we know it all the same. It ain't my call; I just did you a favour seeing Dooley. So, Detective, what are you going to do about it?"

I think you might say that Jastrow left later with a sore head. I believe he cursed me and Egan a few times, somewhat more with each full glass that he demanded and emptied. I couldn't say I blamed him. Before he went, he suggested the obvious – going straight to Lieutenant Hendrik, his boss at the precinct.

"Uh huh. He don't like me," I said.

"You're wrong; he hates you. He thinks you're a no-good bum. He could be right. But he's straight, as straight as they come."

I believed it, actually, so I nodded. "Ok. But he won't take it if he knows it comes from me. When you see him, don't mention me. What do you think he will do?"

14

"He'll say there really ain't nothing to go on…or he'll tell me to contact Brooklyn and pass it back to them. He might surprise me with something else." Jastrow suddenly sat up; a couple of thoughts had stabbed their way through the bourbon. "I think you should go and see this Byrnes."

"Oh?"

"And I'll find out more about Dooley and where he fits in."

I looked at the clock on the wall – you'd have thought it was art deco if it hadn't been so cheap. I saw that it was too late to argue…about four bourbons too late…and I sighed. "Get outta here. I'll see Byrnes."

*

The Eagle had never quite got over Brooklyn losing its city status. The paper was happy as a clam when the Bridge joined Brooklyn with Manhattan, and then turned sour as a lemon when the city was downgraded to a New York borough. From what I'd heard, circulation was still high and they had the editors and the reporters, like Byrnes, who knew how to keep readers. *'Whatever helps Brooklyn helps the Eagle'* was in the reporters' handbook. It worked both ways: the Borough and the paper had each other's backs.

In downtown Brooklyn, next morning, the bronze eagle above the door of the building near Borough Hall stopped me from walking past. I stood and looked at it for a second and thought about the guy I was going to see. When I rang him, Byrnes hadn't sounded the retiring kind – but not in a way I disliked. He was taking on crooks and cops with a smile and a snarl so some chutzpah was in order. I was tempted to tell him what I knew over the phone but what was that? A cross through his name. I knew what that could mean but he would have laughed. I had the feeling he was going to do that anyway because if he was as smart as he sounded, he would have already figured he was in at the deep end; perhaps he was someone who had scruples, for once, and didn't care who knew it.

I was taken up to an open office that looked like it was filled with people who didn't rest. There was the beetle-wing clatter of typewriter keys and the persistent ringing of bells; when the telephones were finally answered the guys were short, sharp or sarcastic until they heard something that they liked, then they

15

scribbled like crazy or shouted across the room. Each of them was after a Pulitzer Prize and somehow knew they wouldn't get it. A guy came along who looked confident that he might, shook my hand and nodded me in the direction of a side room, shabby, with windows looking out at the office, but quieter.

Byrnes was small and wiry, laid back but full of something; I had the awful feeling that something was called 'guts'. Because he had it, I knew my trip over the river was going to be wasted but that made it seem more important for me to say something to him. He was about my age but that wasn't the only reason I could tell that, like me, he'd seen things in action he hadn't wanted to and fought for things that might not have meant much when he began – but did now. I briefly wondered if he saw in my eyes the same that I saw in his but I laid straight in.

"Thank you for seeing me, Mr. Byrnes. I gotta tell you something, you know?"

He smiled a smile that looked genuine. "Well, I hope so, Mr. Baum. I'm kind of busy. I got a story to write."

"Uh huh. And you know that's the reason I'm here."

"Well, I figured when you rang me." He laughed. "What are you, an honorary cop or something? Haven't you heard, I ain't their flavour of the month."

"I heard. There are always bad apples, Mr. Byrnes."

He nodded. "It's the bad ones I'm after."

"For what it's worth, I think you should keep after them. I'm just here to tell you that if you do, I've heard it may cost you."

"You heard this from who?"

I shook my head. "Can't tell you that. It wasn't from the horse's mouth, but perhaps close enough to it to take seriously."

"What do you want me to say, Mr. Baum?" He hesitated, then suddenly stood up and looked out at the bustling buds in the office. He seemed kind of proud of them, as if they were part of what he thought was good about Brooklyn. I wasn't so sure myself. At last, he said: "Look, my final feature is out in three days. It's going to blow a few things wide open and everything I've got is going to the District Attorney's office. After that…"

"Yeah?"

He laughed again and I started to like the guy even more. "I'm going on holiday for a while."

"Up till then?"

"I'll be working hard and keeping my head down. Three days, that's all."

I picked my hat up off the table and stood up myself. "There's nothing more to be said, Mr. Byrnes, except that I'm kinda worried about you."

He thought for a second. "P.I., aren't you?"

"Uh huh."

"Do you mind what work you do?"

"Anything legal that doesn't get me killed."

"Well, I can't guarantee that – but how would you like to help keep me safe for a few days?"

It shook me that for a second or two I considered taking up that crazy proposition. But instead, I said: "I ain't no escort, Mr. Byrnes. Besides, you look tough enough. Where did you serve?"

"Okinawa, amongst other places. You look tough too, Mr. Baum, and you have principles."

I laughed. "Maybe I have, but they change with my mood. Be safe, Mr. Byrnes."

Out on the street, the wind was blowing chills in my direction across East River. I was feeling cold on the outside and kind of flat inside and I figured a coffee and a pastrami on rye might do something, I didn't know what. I found a deli on Joralemon Street with some tables and a pay phone and while I waited for my sandwich, with extra mustard and two sour dills on the side, I phoned Jastrow. When he answered I filled him in on my meeting.

"What did you think he was going to do, give up his story?" Jastrow said.

"I guess not. In fact, I told him to keep right on at it – just to be careful while he did."

"Where are you?"

I told him and he said, "Well, here's the thing. Egan called me to get the lowdown on the Dooley meet; I gave it to him as you gave it to me. He didn't sound surprised when I told him you'd gone in my place but he wants to hear it all from you. And about Byrnes. Why not? Catch up; jaw. His precinct is a few blocks from you. He may be able to tell you more about Dooley too. Hang loose there, I'll call and see if he's free."

17

"Sure." From the payphone I watched my food arrive and nodded to the waitress. She smiled like she actually meant it and put the coffee down softly; from here it looked like good coffee and I was pleased she didn't spill it.

Jastrow came back on the line. "He's on his way."

"He doesn't want me to go to the precinct?" I asked.

"He's gotta eat, don't he? Enjoy."

"Wait. What about Hendrick?"

I knew Jastrow was scowling when he said that the lieutenant was giving it all some thought. He put the phone down and I sat and ate and gave it all some thought too. What was there to think about? I'd warned Byrnes and it was up to him, the cops, the crooks and the DA what happened next. It was time I got back to earning peanuts while following monkeys.

Egan arrived and I couldn't help smiling, just because it was good to see him. I noticed his navy- blue fleece bulged out at his gut and when he took his cap off, the hair he'd had a few years ago was thinner and greyer. But I wasn't fooled by the sunny uncle look; I'd seen him in action during and after the war.

We shook hands and ordered more coffee and a very large corned beef sandwich for him. I was impolite enough to say that a sergeant's pay suited his lifestyle and he laughed. "It's never enough, Baum. Now, spill the latest on Byrnes. The captain wants to know."

"Captain?"

"Shark. The Sharkster."

I shrugged and told him all I knew, which was actually little.

"And Dooley warned you that Byrnes has had the finger put on him? You sure?"

"He didn't come out with it direct...but I'm sure."

"And Byrnes?"

I said that Byrnes wasn't the sort of guy to stop something once he started. Then, I asked Egan whether some kind of protection for Byrnes might be in order.

"Are you kidding? The Sharkster ain't wasting men on the say so of a stoolie or on someone running down the force."

I shook my head. "That's a pity," I said. "Can you tell me about Dooley?"

"Only what I told Jastrow. Nothing. What did he look like?"

18

I told him about the cool, on-the-level eyes and the scar on his neck.

"Scar, huh?" He stroked his chin and smeared corned beef down it. Finally, he said: "Forget it. He's probably just a small-time runner after a few extra bucks, is all."

"Uh huh." I didn't tell him that Dooley nearly spat in my face when I offered those bucks.

I'd like to say after that Egan and me jawed about old times – but when those times ain't anything but bullets and blood it wasn't a conversation that appealed. So, we spoke about wives (his – I ain't got one), girlfriends (I was one down in that department too), beer, the Dodgers and the Giants while he had a second sandwich.

Then he stood up and put out his hand. We shook. He was serious when he looked me in the eye and said: "I'd say you've done your bit, Baum. It's police business now, one way or the other. Don't get involved. It really ain't worth it."

Before I could say "Uh huh" he turned away and when he opened the door a cold blast of Brooklyn air bullied the steam away from my third cup of coffee. When he'd gone, I watched it settle down again. Then I went to the pay phone.

"Is that the Eagle? Put me through to Mr. Byrnes. Yeah…Byrnes? How much do you pay for babysitting?"

*

They came for Byrnes on the very first night I was staying with him.

He had some nice rooms on the ground floor of a house on the north side of Prospect Park, not snazzy but tidy at least. The streets were of the quiet kind. In the day neighbours stopped to talk at front doors; washing hung between houses; stoops were cleaned off by women whilst minding their babies; teenagers laughed outside the candy stores. I noticed how unguarded everyone was, as if menace in the city did not exist. I envied their indifference.

I met Byrnes at the end of his working day, which was a long one; it was Wednesday and he was safe until evening in the office, surrounded by hacks. We strolled from The Eagle entrance to a bar he knew and had a beer. There was nothing awkward about it; I took it as another job, not one I was used to, but I figured I could handle it for a few days. Besides which, I liked the guy and what he stood for.

His editor wanted some professional heavies to keep an eye on him but he told him he had it in hand and made him offer me sixty dollars for every day I kept him alive, at least until the story was out. I decided to stick to my usual rate just to prove to myself I had principles after all, so I took forty dollars a day, a beer, a burger and a couch to sleep on. Did I really think anything sinister was on the cards? I guess I did, otherwise I wouldn't have been there.

I don't like guns now, but I have one. To keep me safe on some pretty mean streets I rely on being six-one and 190 pounds; a blackjack helps when required. I took both anyway. After our beer we drove my car a few blocks to Byrnes' apartment where we passed the evening talking and sharing bourbon but being careful with it. What he didn't know about Brooklyn wasn't worth the light. He was more than happy to share it all with me apart from exactly what he knew about Oscar Grossman, and the cops; he had to keep some things to himself. We also kept off the subject of war.

I was already awake when the window was quietly broken at 2 a.m. It was expertly done; I sleep light and I might have missed it if I'd not already been turning over things in my mind that made me uneasy. I raised my head slowly from the pillow and found that Byrnes was already standing at the end of the couch; he was just a shadow but still looked as alert as a cat. He put a finger to his lips and then nodded for me to stand behind the door. I saw the outline of the revolver he was carrying and hoped he wouldn't have to use it. The blackjack in my hand felt solid and heavy.

There was more than one of them, I could tell. It turned out there were three; I guess they figured that would be more than enough to deal with a single Brooklyn reporter. They didn't know there were two of us and, more than that, we were veterans and armed; they should have done their homework. An apartment in downtown New York wasn't a Pacific jungle but the instincts for survival were just the same. We were scared, but that was just as we should be; it made us think faster and act

20

quicker. The first of them found that out when he burst through the door. By now his eyes would have adjusted to the darkness, so he could see Byrnes straight ahead of him, but he didn't see my blackjack when I hit him across the nose. I figured that would have broken it but I wasn't worried for him as he was probably ugly enough already to stand a little extra.

The second guy stumbled against the first and Byrnes pistol-whipped him before he could get any further. Then I heard another, and I pressed the light switch. I was right about being ugly but saw that it wasn't just the one – they all had faces only their mothers could love and the one at the front was holding his nose and bleeding like a pig.

I'd like to say that we fully whipped them and made a citizen's arrest but the third guy swung a fist and caught me on the side of the face, the sort of thing that would make anyone mad. Sometimes that helps in a fight, but here I waded in and got tangling with him. The one with the broken nose took advantage and staggered out of the door and I could see Byrnes covering the one he had hit with his pistol. I was annoyed that he had on a tight smile and seemed to be appreciating my footwork. I nearly turned to scowl at him, which was a mistake because I was punched to the stomach and pushed backwards into Byrnes. He and I did a kind of fandango together and when we had finished dancing, saw the heels of the last goon make it out through the door. I moved to go after him but Byrnes put a hand on my arm and shook his head; he still had on his little smile and I swear to God he was enjoying himself.

"Thanks for the help," I growled.

He laughed, then switched off the light and quickly moved to the window. "I think you had it in hand." He pulled the curtain aside so that he could see the street. White light from the corner lamp shone on broken beer glass; the room was a mess.

I heard the slam of vehicle doors and the squealing of tires. "I think we should call the cops now."

"Don't bother," he said.

I hurried to the window and saw the tail-lights of two cars turn the corner out of sight. I could swear that one of them was a police cruiser.

We cleaned up and Byrnes did a pretty good omelette with mozzarella for breakfast a few hours later. After some strong coffee, we ran things past each other.

"You notice they didn't use shooters?" Byrnes asked me.

"Perhaps we didn't give them a chance," I said.

"No. They weren't going to hurt me."

"Oh." I rubbed the side of my face.

"I mean, they weren't going to hurt me…right then."

"Meaning?"

"They want to know how much I know and who else I've told. Whether I have that information put by, and where. Most of all, they want to know if there's a way they can stop me from spilling the beans."

"I think we know how they can do that."

He laughed the sort of laugh that filled me with confidence; I needed it after our early morning fracas. Byrnes was the kind of guy that looked life in the eye and took all the bad things it offered on the chin. Then he laughed back at it. I remembered how he was wearing that little smile while we rumbled.

"I guess they are dumber than I thought," he said.

"How so?"

"A lot of what I know is up here, sure." He tapped his forehead. "But names, records, papers…they're safe. And if they're *really* dumb and think by getting rid of me it's all going away…it ain't. My editor knows almost as much as I do."

"It seems like you and he are putting yourself on the line. If it goes as you want, they ain't going to be happy; you could be looking over your shoulder for a long time."

He laughed again. "My editor will risk anything for the biggest story in New York."

"That big?"

He went serious and cynical on me. "It's big. You might be a little disappointed in this great city of ours."

"The city never disappoints me," I said, "just the people in it."

He sipped his coffee slowly. "I owe someone something. You, for being here…"

"I'm getting paid."

"...and whoever it was gave us the tip. Will you tell me who it was?"

I thought about it, then figured there may be something to be gained in telling him who had saved his bacon. "Yes. Name's Dooley. Patrick. A Brooklynite, I figure. If you know the name and he's on your list...well, you might give him a break."

Slowly, he leaned back in his chair. He nodded. "I know a Dooley... or at least I did. By Jesus...Patrick Dooley...?"

"That's the name. What does it mean to you?"

He was quiet for a few moments. Then: "If it's the same, he was shelled at Kakazu Ridge, and I dragged him away from the line of fire."

I didn't interrupt the silence straight away; he was thinking of things he didn't want to think about. From what I'd heard it was wave after Japanese wave, mostly at night. Finally, I said: "I guess he figures you are even now."

Byrnes roused himself and looked at me a little strangely. "Yes. Yes...I guess he would. The only thing is, he's dead."

*

I needed bringing down to earth and the cat needed feeding so, when it got light, and Byrnes had left for The Eagle, I drove home. I walked through the door and the cat looked at me aggrieved, like he was missing our nightly games of chess, but I explained the situation and drank some coffee as he ate – it didn't seem to bother him none what I had been up to. Then, I figured it was time to pay a visit to the office and make some phone calls; I needed to get a few things straight. I suppose it was the Dooley thing; after last night, I was worried about him – no one likes a fink. Still, you can't kill a dead man, can you?

If the mood takes me, and I need time to think, I like to walk a distance then take the subway from 137th. The synagogue on Old Broadway sometimes draws me and if I ain't careful one day I'll go in. Today, Rabbi Jakob was on the step opening up and for once I didn't try to avoid him. "Shalom, Rabbi."

He smiled and tried not to look surprised. "Ah, shalom, shalom, Aaron. Such a long time. Your mother, your *ima* – may her memory be blessed – would be disappointed in you were she still with us."

23

"Rabbi, she was disappointed in me when she *was* with us."

He spread the doors open as wide as they would go. "Are you sure you won't…?"

"I'd only clutter up the place, Rabbi. Say…how do we stand on resurrection?"

"Aaron, all will rise in the World to Come."

"Yeah. What about in this world?"

He gave a laugh and shook his head. "You have been reading the wrong scriptures, Aaron."

"Just how I figured it." I left him looking after me as if I was some *schmuck* that needed guidance; he was right, of course.

I wasn't expecting to beat off any paying clients waiting outside the office, and I was right. There was a note on the door from Rosie, the typist along the corridor: '*Collect your own post, dumbass.*' I could tell she had a thing for me so, after I entered, I kept it for two seconds before I threw it in the bin, then made for the phone book.

The drawing I'd bought of a dark-haired beauty hung framed and in shadow on the wall but her eyes still followed me to my desk and watched as I looked through the pages. I stopped at Dooley; there were 47 of them in Brooklyn but only one Patrick, and a P.B. I dialled the obvious one first. While I waited, I looked at the new light shade and wondered if it was all looking too classy. I didn't want the landlord to raise the rent.

You could say I struck lucky – but only in that the phone picked up at the first ring. As soon as he spoke, I knew it wasn't the guy from the bar, who had been polite enough until he got annoyed at me.

"Mr. Dooley? Mr. Patrick Dooley?"

"Yeah. Who wants to know?" he growled. I put the phone down.

P.B. Dooley turned out to be a fish-mongers. That left me discussing the merits of flaky cod for a few moments before I could say goodbye; it also left me high and dry as far as Dooleys were concerned.

Then, Jastrow rang. "Baum?"

"Sure."

"Meet me at the city morgue."

"Why so?"

"A stiff turned up last night not far from the Elm Bar."

I tried not to narrow my eyes. "Do I know every stiff in Manhattan?" I said.

"You might know this one. He has a shrapnel scar on his neck."

*

The morgue ain't somewhere you want to go for a day out. January was still cold and spitting flakes but the morgue would be colder still – it has to be. Before I left the office, I rang Byrnes and told him to get down to Bellevue. He was about to argue until I told him why; then the phone went dead, and I figured within thirty seconds he'd be in his car clipping it over the Brooklyn Bridge. I took the subway and watched mid-week workers coming on or off shifts; their faces told me which.

When I arrived Jastrow and a cop in uniform were waiting. We left the cop at reception for Byrnes and headed to the hospital basement. Any challenge was met with a flash of Jastrow's badge and at the bottom of the stairs was a doorway to a waiting room, purely for the living, and another to the morgue itself. Outside that door was one of the medical examiners looking bored and trying not to, but still professional as heck. He asked for I.D., then took us in. A gurney stood there with somebody shorn of life lying on it under a sheet. For some reason there is always a pause before the sheet is pulled back and the M.E. didn't disappoint us; he waited a second then uncovered the face.

Jastrow raised his eyebrows and looked at me, and I looked at the face. The eyes were not as lively as when I had seen them last; they lacked that sense of indignation which between then and now I had decided I liked. Now, they were just dead and cold as hell.

"Yeah. That's Dooley," I said.

The door behind us swung open and the cop came in with Byrnes alongside. The cop looked young and nervous. Byrnes didn't look it, but he was too; it ain't often you hear of a man who died twice. He stood above the man and the lights, which were making my head ache, were bright enough to show every line on the face looking blankly up at them. The scars on his neck, I could see, reached further down below the sheets. They were made by the sorts of shrapnel that would have made a man

25

scream but not be heard amongst many others in the theater of war.

I wasn't sure what I expected but Byrnes took a good, long look then shook his head. "That ain't Dooley. At least, it's not the Dooley I know."

We all looked at each other and then Jastrow turned to the M.E. "What's the cause of death, Doc?"

The M.E. lifted his glasses onto his forehead. "There is a stab wound to the aorta – that's the one, but several others to the abdomen and lower back. To me, it seems he was intended to die…but not easily."

Jastrow nodded. "Let's go have a coffee and talk," he said.

I let the others go and took a final look at Dooley…or whoever. It didn't matter why he'd told me that was his name, though I intended to find out. It mattered that he took a chance on doing the right thing. It mattered that he was now presented as a lesson to others who might also want to do the right thing. It mattered that he was younger than me…and deader.

We found a coffee bar nearby that looked like it served something worth the name and Jastrow put it to Byrnes. "Tell us about Dooley. Are you sure that ain't him?"

"The only resemblance is that they are both dead. I was a corporal; he was a private. I saved his life, but not for long. He was in the field hospital for two weeks and I thought he was going to make it…but no, he's gone, Detective."

A few wheels began turning but I said nothing and Jastrow moved on. "The thing is this, Byrnes. One man is dead and there could have been another; that's you. Is your story worth it? Bribery and corruption is one thing; homicide is another and that's my thing. Baum here likes to think he's tough…"

"He is."

"…but can't you just hand your stuff over to the D.A. now? I figure they could subpoena it anyway."

"I'll just deny it exists…two more days, Detective. Brooklyn…New York…deserves to know what lies in its belly."

"Then if you are staying at home, you need protection. I'll contact Captain Shark. I'm sure he'll be happy to arrange something for you."

Byrnes slowly smiled his stiff little smile. "I'm pretty sure he would."

Jastrow looked at him but before he could say anything, I chipped in. "Byrnes can stay with me."

Jastrow shrugged. "If your cat is happy with it, so am I. I'm asking Lieutenant Hendricks to put two men of our own on the street, though."

We both nodded and Byrnes stood up to go. When he had left for his office, I asked Jastrow how long it would take to find out who the dead man was.

"That depends. Missing Persons might have a report already. If he has a wife who loves him, not long."

I thought back to our meeting. "He'll have a wife," I said.

*

That evening, Byrnes and I sat drinking beer at my place. The cat welcomed him then mewled when he challenged me to a game of chess but settled down to watch, and it turned out he wasn't bad. Outside on the street a squad car sat reassuring us a little but, as we played, I was thinking hard. Perhaps that's why it took fifteen moves to check mate him. It occurred to me that Byrnes would have his story; he was gearing up for the Saturday Eagle, the city would have more grievances to air and people would howl – but with what Byrnes had they would get satisfaction from knowing that certain crooks, and those that supported them in low and high places, would get their just desserts. It wasn't enough for me; it should have been but it wasn't. Not since someone had come for me and Byrnes and failed, and others had gone for 'my' Dooley and succeeded. I put it to Byrnes that these events were considered attempted kidnap on the one hand and homicide on the other.

"Yeah. That's what they are. And there ain't any evidence of who did either."

"It was Grossman, of course. And others with a lot to lose."

"Sure."

"Well...illegal gambling, bribery, corruption – it's a roll call alright. Some crooks and cops will go in the slammer...but maybe not for long. Murder deserves more, doesn't it?" I decided on something I'd been mulling over. "You know," I said, "I don't

27

even know who is on this list of yours. It's about time you showed me – you owe me a preview before the papers hit the stands."

Byrnes nodded. "I guess I do." He had already worked this one out, because he went to the coat stand, which pretended to look all art deco, and took a manilla envelope from the inside pocket of his jacket. I was surprised how small it was and I must have shown it because he laughed. "I typed this up for you," he said. "It don't take much space for two or three dozen names or so. Our incorruptible police force." He looked at me and said: "There are some names you might be interested in..."

I took the list. There were many that I didn't recognise and some that I did. I whistled at the names of several precinct commanders and at least two assistant chiefs. This would all come crashing down and it wouldn't be good for those higher up the chain either – whether they knew what was going on or not. I saw Captain Shark on the list. Then, beneath that, the name I was looking for and never wanted to see.

"Tomorrow there is something I need to do," I said.

We finished our beers and I tossed Byrnes a blanket and a pillow so he could be more comfortable on a couch that was slightly too small for him. I left him with the lamp on and went to the bedroom and when I turned at the door, I saw that lamp throwing out amber light on a bare space on the wall. I'd never really noticed it before and I wondered how a space like that could make a room feel so desolate when it had a guest and a cat in it. I figured I needed to buy another picture.

*

In what used to be called Cobles Hill in South Brooklyn there were plenty of nice-looking row houses for those that could afford them. If you were one of those that couldn't it was possible to rent a whole floor or two, but at a price still way above what people were willing to pay me. The next day, I pulled up outside one of them, brownstone and clean, climbed the steps and knocked. Egan answered the door with a hot dog in his hand and ketchup round his mouth at 9:00 a.m.

He looked nervous when he saw me but managed to hide most of that by taking a mouthful of dog and trying to smile at the same time. He wiped one hand on his trousers before holding it out and when he had swallowed gave me a chummy welcome. "Baum! Once in two years not enough for you? Come on in, buddy, come in."

I grinned and stepped across the porch. "Nice place you have here. I should have stayed in the force."

"Yeah...well, it's just the one floor but...say, what can I do for you?"

"Yeah, still, it's nice...is your wife in?"

He looked surprised. "Why, no, she's just out at..."

"That's fine," I said.

I gave him the hardest punch in the mouth I could. It wasn't enough. I remembered how tough Egan was, someone I was always pleased to have next to me in conflict – and though he staggered he stayed upright and made sure he didn't drop his hot dog, so I hit him again. This time he and the dog and the ketchup landed on a good-looking rug.

"I won't ask you why you got involved. I'm sure your wife is pretty, perhaps hard to please, and who don't want to haul themselves up the greasy ladder?" I gazed around at the hall, pleasant and airy and expensive. "But did Dooley have to be killed?"

He rubbed his chin. "Are you crazy? Do you think I had anything to do with that?"

"You told Grossman who it was finked on him. On what they were going to do to Byrnes."

"I told Shark, yeah, he asked me to find out but..."

"What did you think they would do to a snitch, Egan?"

He went quiet. I like to think he hated himself; to be honest I think he did. "Not that...no... not that," he said softly.

"What was his real name?"

"Minahan. Liam Minahan. We'd never heard of no Dooley but as soon as I told Shark about the scars on his neck, he recognised him as a small-time runner and hanger on for Grossman. That was all I did."

"Apart from taking kick-backs and turning a blind eye to Grossman's illegal activities?" I almost sneered but I needed to keep Egan on board. "This could be 'aiding a murder', for you."

"You know that ain't me, Baum. You and me and Jastrow…we're brothers…brothers in arms."

I thought back to '44 and '45. It was true and I nodded. "That's why I'm here, Egan," I said softly. "I'm giving you a chance to do the right thing. Minahan was a brother too. Where else would he get those scars? I need you to come with me and tell the truth. Are you going to do it?"

It took him a long time. Thinking about the future, weighing it up; looking at the past too, regretting lots of it.

Finally, he said: "Yes…yes, I'll do it."

I held out my hand and pulled him up. "Go get your coat."

*

The Saturday edition of The Eagle had five inside pages full of the sort of stuff people love to get riled about; in this case with good reason. Byrnes had hit the spot with his report and carried the whole city's anger with him on this. It wasn't just illegal gambling; he had enough inside dope on the NYPD to make it sound rife with corruption. It wasn't, but it was plenty, and with what he spilled and had sent to the D.A. I could see the mayor himself falling on his sword.

More important to me was the front-page picture of Oscar Grossman and Captain Shark cuffed and arrested for the murder of one Liam Minahan. It was the first time I had laid eyes on either of them and both lived up to their names: the crook looked large and fat, the cop was lean and predatory. They both looked unhappy. I hoped they would take the chair in Sing Sing.

That afternoon, I shook hands with Byrnes outside his office and congratulated him. "I think you've done New York a service, and perhaps yourself if that Pulitzer comes your way."

"I didn't do it for that, you know?"

"I know," I said as I walked towards my car.

"I should be coming with you," he called out.

"No, this is something I'd like to do by myself," I said. I turned around and nodded to him. "Take that holiday. You've earned it."

*

30

At Canarsie, near Jamaica Bay, were several hundred Quonset huts where ex-servicemen were housed; Cobles Hill it wasn't. It threw me back eight years and I could have been at the barracks. I almost felt the Pacific heat and sun though Brooklyn was still wrapped in ice and I, in turn, was wrapped up against it. Still, I took off my hat and let the cold wind muss my hair when the door was answered at number 32; the woman who stood there wasn't in mourning dress but was grieving just the same. Her head was uncovered and the blackness of her hair was only a little darker than her eyes and the circles beneath them.

"Mrs. Minahan?"

"Yes."

"My name's Baum. I knew your husband...a little," I said.

She wasn't sure about it, but said: "Won't you come in?"

The place was poorly furnished but small and neat, which seemed to sum up Mrs. Minahan too, except she was pretty, and when she managed to smile in her grief, she looked even prettier. She was quietly spoken and she had a slight Irish accent like her husband.

I came clean early on that I'd only met her husband once – and how, where and why. I wasn't sure what she knew about who her husband had hung out with, but she seemed to sense that.

"Liam was a good man, Mr. Baum...if you can't find work and someone offers you money..."

"I ain't making judgment, Mrs. Minahan. He saved Mr. Byrnes' life and paid the price himself. Did he know a Patrick Dooley by any chance?"

"Patrick Dooley? Why, yes, he did. They were friends, Mr. Baum. He knew him before and during the war and he was with him when he died."

"In hospital? Were they together at the hospital in Okinawa?"

"That's what he told me when he returned home."

She offered me coffee, which I accepted, and we both drank slowly and quietly. Then I rose and offered her goodbyes and condolences in return. We shook hands at the door. Her hand was soft; her face was pale and that black hair moved around in the wind.

31

I made for the office and picked something up, then headed home. While I drove, I got it straight in my head; I had it figured now as best I could.

Dooley didn't make it; we all know that now. But perhaps when he knew he was dying in the hospital, he told Minahan to thank Byrnes for trying to save his life. Minahan went one better – he saw the chance, years down the line, to warn Byrnes that Grossman was coming after him. Here's another 'perhaps': he used Patrick Dooley's name so that Byrnes knew a debt was being repaid. Or, it may just have been that he couldn't use his own name because a bad thing would happen to him. It did anyway.

When I walked in, my apartment was quiet, just how I liked it. The cat woke and purred a little and watched while I filled the space on the wall with the drawing I'd taken from the office; straight away the room felt kind of intimate. Outside, Manhattan darkened and at least some of it slept. I drank three bourbons as I sat, warm and heavy-eyed, while the woman in the drawing looked at me, and I, her; she danced and swirled in front of me and just before I closed my eyes, I was thinking that she seemed to be every woman I'd ever known.

Aaron Baum P.I. was first introduced in the short story: "The Lady in the Room" from "Light and Dark: 21 short stories", available on Amazon.

C.G. Harris is currently writing a series of Aaron Baum stories entitled: "The Casebook of Aaron Baum" which is due for release in time for Easter 2022.

THE GENTLE GIANT

By Glynne Covell

My life is ebbing away; I know it. My strength is seeping slowly from my body, like water evaporating from a dried-up stream. I know it. Time is the enemy; the one indestructible power no one on earth can control. Time is running out and acceptance of this fate is paramount to peace of mind. To fight the reality of death is futile.

I was born in 1973 in the south of Sudan, staying with my mother for nearly three years. Gradually weaned and guided in survival tactics to independence in this beautiful world, I spent happy days foraging for our herbivorous diet of fruits, stems, twigs, grasses and leaves. Under the watchful eye of my mother, I learnt to stay safe from the danger of crocodiles, big cats and wild dogs. Those enemies target the calves. Fortunately, we can move fast to escape hazardous situations. Eating is easy living on the savannah; it is not difficult to find places to graze and despite a lack of teeth at the front, my square lips suck up food easily. But there was no place to hide, nowhere to run to escape man. The real danger. I was far from ready for the separation in 1975, which came when I was wrenched from my protectorate by men. Poachers. I do not know my mother's fate but mine was a manhandling, terrifying and painful transit from my home to a zoo in Czechoslovakia. I was drugged, imprisoned for endless days. Pointless to struggle. This enemy was mightily powerful.

There is pain. Great pain in my joints. I cannot stand. Eating is difficult now. Slowly, slowly, I am becoming weaker as I lie here and think back on my life.

My name is Sudan, but I am also known as Gentle Giant. I am a northern white rhino. Some mistakenly believe I am quite white, but the word 'white' has come about from the term 'wyd' in Afrikaans, which means wide. I grew to be six feet tall, weighing 5,000 pounds and yes, I am wide.

The zoo I was taken to was basic but fulfilled my needs in order to live. But not my need to mentally survive. That was a slow decline. We are semi social animals and rather territorial,

33

females being more adaptable whereas males are more solitary. That did not help my plight. Zoos are unnatural habitats for us to thrive, mentally and physically. Claustrophobic, monotonous and predictable. Torturous. I know my brain is small, but it is large enough to feel and deserve freedom. All beings need freedom. It is an earthly right. I grew, it is true. My horn especially. Whereas I kept mine, I often wondered if Mother was killed for hers. Man demands big money, as much as gold, for these tusks of keratin, which are ground up and used for medicine. My poachers had been encouraged by a circus and my role in the zoo was to breed. Here, I survived until 2009 and in fact, I sired two females. That was my role but after the dawn of the new century, sadly there were no more calves. Numbers were decreasing at a most alarming rate.

I sleep, I wake. I feel pain with every breath. There is no more energy in my body to carry on living.

With my breeding days over, I was taken back to the African habitat where I was born, along with my offspring. Conservationists hoped that the Ol Pejeta Conservancy would encourage breeding, but sadly, this was not meant to be. The natural death of another male in 2014 awarded me the title of the only surviving male of the northern whites. The evolutionary thread was left with me. Poaching had interfered disastrously with our survival.

Here I am, struggling to breath, my heart beginning to fail. I am cherished here. Revered. I have a transmitter embedded in my horn. There are watch towers, fences and drones around me and trained, armed guards protecting my existence. It seems that some people realised and respected the lives of my species, but sadly not enough. Profiteering, short-term thinking men destroy and cut the evolutionary chain which has existed for millions of years.

I am motionless. My breathing is shallow, ragged. A kindly keeper at my side caresses my old leather-like skin. He seems sad. I can see he is crying. He is giving me something to ease my suffering. Gentle man. Compassionate human. Not only do I suffer with degenerative changes in my muscles and bones, but my skin now has extensive and spreading sores. It is 2018. I am 45 but to man that is akin to 90.

One more breath and...peace.

So ends the time on earth of the northern white rhino. Gone. Finished. A crime if ever there was one.

ALICE AND THE WHITE RABBIT

By Janet Winson

I brought the call to an abrupt end as I heard Solly's key turn in the lock and quickly finished my conversation. "Okay, Joyce, see you at about a quarter to eight tomorrow morning then. Full English at Maggie's. I'll be looking out for the car." I replaced the receiver and realised that I'd been chewing at my finger nails while chatting.

The front door slammed and there in the doorway stood Solly, holding onto the door frame to steady himself. The pungent smell of beer mingled with tobacco smoke, held together by the usual wet overcoat odour; it became overwhelming and I turned away.

"Where's my dinner, girl?" He sat heavily on the settee by the TV and shrugged off his coat. Bending to undo his suede Hush Puppies, he pulled them off, aiming them towards the corner. His height always seemed manageable when he was sitting down and I remembered when he used to call me his 'Pocket Venus' back in the early days. That illusion was long gone, and I automatically scuttled into the kitchenette and extricated the shepherd's pie from the oven, noticing it was going black on the corners. As usual he was home late and I, as usual, had enjoyed my dinner alone three hours earlier. I put the plate down on the table beside the waiting cutlery, which included a spoon as there always had to be some 'afters'. Solly had a sweet tooth and a sour manner and I was tired but accustomed to life being like this. As I waited for the expected grumble about the meal, I silently counted down: "Five, four, three, two, one and then..."

"Alice, what have you done to the dinner, girl? You've cremated it. I'll need plenty of brown sauce to take the taste away."

I disappeared upstairs, disguising my anger and leaving him to it. Within a few minutes I could hear him banging the poor sauce bottle and muttering.

I recovered by deliberately concentrating on the next day, out with my oldest and best friend, Joyce, who had Fridays off. I planned to wear my favourite coat although it had now seen better days; at least it still fitted, and I loved the shawl collar. Earlier on I had raided the Horlicks jar where the Christmas cash was stashed away. Solly would have to like it or lump it tomorrow. I didn't know what he had been up to all day and after all this time I didn't care either; to be dramatic, my tears had run dry years ago. Two Valium pills replaced a custard cream to go with my evening cup of tea. Comfortably propped up and reading in the bedroom, I could soon hear Solly snoring away in front of the television and I found my earplugs. He wouldn't disturb me again tonight.

The front door slammed at 6.30 a.m. as Solly Jnr. left for his early shift in an engineering firm at Tower Bridge. At 17, this was his first job and he cycled in every day with a packed lunch. Solly Junior, the only good thing from our 25 years together; as a youngster he always tended to be a mother's boy and had become increasingly wary of his father since he reached adolescence. It was obvious to me that he was hating factory work and I was painfully aware that before too long his father would find him something different, less ordinary, seedy and on the edge and the thought of this was breaking my heart.

In the bathroom, Solly was shaving noisily, late as usual. He always had people to meet around the market or dock offices. We had a sideboard full of top-quality cigars and branded liquor, no questions asked.

As I was dozing off again, Solly's head popped round the bedroom door; he looked hungover but smartly turned out as ever. "See you tonight, girl. Got to see a man about a dog down Dockhead. Fancy a new leather coat for Christmas? The Borge brothers are expecting a load of coats this weekend from Malta. Let me know what colour you want. Got to get me skates on now!"

The door banged and he had gone.

Later, ready to go out, I gazed through the net curtains as Joyce's Hillman Minx, known as 'the limo', perky in turquoise and white and such a beautiful little motor, stopped outside. This was our transport most Fridays. Joyce had always been a career girl, no kids and a husband with a steady job at the bank. She always said she'd had her fill of babies at work and didn't ever want one to take home. I agreed that she had a point: Joyce had been training as a nurse at the time I was first hanging around with Solly and she now worked four days a week as a health visitor. We had been friends since childhood and we met most Fridays for a meal together or a shopping trip.

I was soon climbing into the passenger seat, after moving a box of orange juice and castor oil onto the back seat. I looked at her sitting beside me, her shiny brown hair heavily lacquered and back-combed, sitting high off her forehead. As she released the handbrake, I noticed a new gold wrist watch.

We found a parking spot on a terraced street between the market and some dingy old warehouses. We were near the dockside and could hear the big cranes clunking and the sound of men shouting and vehicles honking, very busy as ever. We made our way to Maggie's. The front windows were opaque with condensation and, as we pushed the door open, the delicious smell of bacon wafted over and immediately my mouth was watering. After fighting our way in through the thick cigarette smoke, there was nowhere to sit down. We decided to leave it half an hour or so as the place was heaving and painfully noisy. We needed enough space and a bit of peace to relax and enjoy a gossip.

"I wonder if there's any stalls still open this time of the morning?" muttered Joyce, patting her hair. We both knew the main Bermondsey Market ran all Thursday night and was usually finishing up by 9.00 a.m. The main trade was in the dark hours, when many a deal was made under the eye of plain clothes police who often found a lovely bargain to take home. The pub just beside the market was open during trading hours and there were still a few dishevelled boozers stumbling about, heading towards the bus stops just down the road.

"Let's have a mooch for half an hour," I suggested, as I spotted two elderly women who were still set up at the far end. They had a variety of knick-knacks: lots of it was brassware, shiny and battered, fire irons, coal scuttles, fire guards, all destined to become defunct as fireplaces were increasingly pine-clad for disguise or badly knocked right out, just leaving a space for a small gas fire. We made a move towards another table that was covered in a red chenille cloth; Joyce, a magpie by nature, had spotted a variety of small, decorative pieces of paste jewellery and pushed me towards it. The smaller lady looked up and cleared her glass of Guinness out of view; The Jolly Sailor was about to close and the pot man was sweeping up outside. The stale smell of spilt beer was strong and reminded me of Solly. I looked in my handbag for a Polo mint.

Joyce was examining a brooch that was set with paste pearls and rubies but the first thing to catch my eye was an old Victorian vase containing what I imagined to be hatpins, something I hadn't seen for at least a decade. I leaned over and started to sort through them. The stall owner saw my interest and began to spin me a story of how her aunts had always kept a hatpin during the blackout to ward off unwanted attention. She went on to tell me about her grandmother, who had been a suffragette and had enjoyed a few adventures with the police. I love a story like that and for some unexplained reason, I decided there and then to choose one or two hatpins, though I only wore a hat at weddings or funerals nowadays. I noticed Joyce was getting out her purse and had bought a double row of old but fake pearls. This prompted me to choose a brooch with a purple thistle and I randomly took a couple of the longest hatpins I could find. The talkative lady wrapped them up in a couple of pages of the Daily Mirror and told me to be careful and not prick my finger getting them out. I thought I had done pretty well for a mere six bob.

We were soon enjoying a nice cup of tea in Maggie's and our full English breakfasts were ordered; the rush was over and we could hear ourselves speak now. Joyce put her hand over mine and said softly: "What's up with your eye, Alice? Has that bugger of a husband been using you as a punchbag again?"

I was shocked as I had spent absolutely ages applying the foundation and Max Factor crème puff before I left home. I realised with dread that her soft tone and concern had now done something to my eyes too; I felt a big tear form and drop into my teacup. I talked it all through with Joyce over the toast and marmalade and she said a few things that made me realise life should be so much better. She offered to help me if I needed it.

*

I opened the wardrobe wide to reveal the long mirror inside the door, then I turned to carry on with my frantic assault on the large parcel left at the end of the bed. I ripped the Christmas paper off and instantly smelt leather, as I had hoped. I pulled the coat out of the torn-up wrapping and with my hands shaking, I slipped the coat on over my nightdress. Giddy with disbelief, I gazed at the beautiful three-quarter leather coat the colour of autumn conkers that, amazingly, matched my hair. The fit was as good as tailored and it really made me look special, even over my nightdress. The mirror was giving me a definite 'thumbs up' and I instantly forgave Solly, who had given me nothing for Christmas but now on 31st December, my 43rd birthday, here was the joint Christmas/birthday present that I had assumed he had only promised as a get-out clause and doubted would ever materialise.

Perhaps Solly still loved me, despite his vile moods over the past month and the black eye that I had probably deserved, burning his food and keeping him out of the bedroom. My inner voice told me that 1964 would be a great year for us. Love had come back at last and the future was going to be so much better. I took off the coat and carefully hung it on one of my best padded hangers. I kept going upstairs every hour or so for the rest of the day just to feast my eyes on the coat and to bask in all that I wanted it to mean.

I spent the day looking through old photos, reliving my early days with Solly as far back as junior school; I had always had my eye on him. He was a real looker back then, tall with an amazing head of blond, almost white hair. His dad had been a Norwegian who had only been around for his conception and had jumped back on his ship after the timber was delivered to the docks; Solly only knew that he came from Bergen. His mother had bravely named him Sven but with the second name of Solomon, after his maternal grandfather. He was never known as Sven but was called Solly from his first days at school and it had stuck.

Solly Smith looked so different from the other boys but just like them, football was his first love. He played for the school team as a winger and was known for his speed and determination. His striking hair and sheer energy resulted in his nickname of 'White Rabbit'; equally, he had no spare fat on him back then.

Solly was soon tall enough to easily get into the local pubs while still well under age and around that time we became a couple, young and far too eager to be grown-ups. It was years later that one of Solly's aunts came up with the 'Alice and White Rabbit' connection; she must have been a bit of a bookworm.

I realised the contradiction at this point: here I was, still waiting for Wonderland, nearly 30 years on. I put my old photos away and by 9.00 p.m. we were stepping out arm in arm towards the local pub three streets down to have a few drinks for New Year's Eve and my birthday. I wore my new coat with total pride and felt like somebody again, the first time for so long. As I wobbled, avoiding the icy puddles in my stilettos, Solly turned and gave me a rare kiss.

"Happy birthday, doll!"

The pub was packed out and noisy. Everybody was already well oiled. Shirley, the landlady's sister was banging out 'Glad All Over' on the battered old upright piano in the corner and the customers were stamping their feet and howling away "…so glad you're mine." The bar staff couldn't fill the glasses quickly enough; beer was flowing freely. I glanced up at the crepe paper chains all twined around the ceiling lights, garish in contrast to the dirty yellow ceiling, and the few surviving balloons now looking sadly deflated, and I felt a sudden sadness for a moment.

Solly found two seats between the dartboard and the door to the gents' and pushed his path through the crowd and up to the bar, quickly coming back with a pint of Best and a Babycham with a cherry on a cocktail stick. It was getting close to midnight now as more punters pushed in through the doors, beer slopping, and everyone now laughing, cheering and all half-cut. Shirley started again, playing the familiar rhythm of the Conga and everyone started forming up to make a line that soon became a snake.

I was steaming hot now, still in my coat, but there was no way I wanted to leave it on the back of my chair. But nobody could resist a Conga on New Year's Eve and I was soon grabbing the well-corseted waist of the landlady and off we went. Three steps and a kick and repeat, through the saloon bar and into the public bar round the front of the pub and back again via the street where it was freezing cold. I had seen Solly behind me but by the time we collapsed back in the bar to finish our drinks and order the next round, he had disappeared.

I immediately smelt trouble but I finished the sticky remains of my drink and threw the cocktail stick into the messy ashtray. I felt a hand on my shoulder and began to relax but instead of Solly, it was Dennis, the pub landlord as he began to clear the table. He noticed my anxious face and bent forward to whisper into my ear. "Your Solly sloped off with Borgy just now. They both looked ready for a bit of a set-to. They went round and out towards the yard."

Dennis inclined his head towards the exit sign opposite. I knew who Dennis meant. Borgy was one of the two local and infamous Borge brothers, notorious for their trips in and out of the local court for trading stolen goods, GBH, and the rest. I immediately cottoned on to the link with my new coat and just felt sick. I made a dash for the saloon bar exit towards the back yard but before I got that far I could hear a rumpus downstairs, coming from the cellar immediately below me. The door to the cellar was unlocked and ajar. I discarded my high heels and, in the semi-darkness, ran down the dirty cellar stairs in my stockinged feet.

The half-light coming through the door threw confusing shadows around me but there was shouting and what appeared to be something shiny moving around just in front of a line of beer barrels. I recognised Borgy, so much taller than Solly and also built like a heavyweight boxer; he was flashing a six-inch knife in front of a half-collapsed Solly who had knocked over a pile of beer crates, leaving a fair amount of spilt beer and broken glass all around him. Even in the poor light it was obvious that Solly had taken a serious beating. His nose poured blood all down his tie and white shirt.

Borgy sensed me standing behind him and turned on me with the knife. He looked me up and down with more hatred than anger, then, sneering at Solly, he spoke right into his face, spittle flying freely. "Oh, I see you nicked a nice coat for your missus while you were at it then? She won't be wearing it again, you thieving bastard."

Borgy turned around and lashed at my coat with his knife, splitting it in several places in fast succession. Next, he grabbed

42

my shoulders and arm and pulled the coat off me very roughly. When he had the coat over his arm, he pushed me hard and I ended up on the floor not too far from Solly, now sitting comatose in a puddle of beer and broken glass, his breathing fast and loud and his eyes closing up already.

Borgy aimed a specific, final hard kick at Solly's lower half and Solly moaned as his head fell onto his chest. "It's not over, don't you worry," muttered Borgy, shaking his head. Then he was gone, and I heard his footsteps going up the cellar steps.

I checked that Solly was still breathing, despite what now looked like a badly broken nose. I was shaking with shock but, most of all, mortified about my coat. I quickly added two and two together, now realising that Solly must have found where the coats were being stored and had probably stolen a number of them to re-sell across the river somewhere. My dream coat been such a good fit and lovely colour but I'd seen the last of it. I looked across at him without pity, only disgust; my heart hardened against him but my brain soon took over again.

Somehow, I pushed Solly up those cellar steps. He was bowed and his legs were letting him down. I found my abandoned high-heels by the door and as we left the cellar, I could hear the chimes of Big Ben loudly coming from the radio in the saloon bar. We left the pub through the backyard and there I stood, supporting Solly in his half-standing position on the freezing, icy pavement. The sentimental words of 'Auld Lang Syne' were in the air. I could imagine them all, hugging and kissing each other in the bar, wishing "Happy New Year" to each other as we waited, Solly moaning from his many injuries and me freezing to death without my leather coat. At that moment I told myself: "It's no use going back to yesterday because you were a different person then."

*

New Year's Day was a Sunday and Solly stayed in bed all morning. His eyes could hardly open and he was still angry rather than sorry. I couldn't bear to look at him or speak to him, but I had to keep up appearances as his mother and aunt were coming over for roast beef and all the trimmings at 2.00 p.m. Solly Jnr. had excused himself for the day. He was staying at his friend's flat in Rotherhithe and had asked me to put his Sunday lunch in the oven for him to eat later. He didn't mention his father, though he must have heard him moaning and cursing all night. My son gave me a quizzical look as he went out, but we never spoke about Solly much; it worked for us as he didn't want to know and I didn't want to tell him anything.

I took my nice green sheath dress and matching cardigan out of the wardrobe, ready to wear when our company arrived, and then began preparing the meal, beating the batter, and putting the joint in the oven. I then gave myself half an hour to tidy myself up, pinning my hair to put in a few curls in the front then tying a favourite silk scarf over my hair to disguise it while my curls 'took'. I decided to put on a bit of make-up; I looked such a sight with my pale face. I found my old biscuit tin in the bedroom where I kept various pieces of costume jewellery and bits and pieces and there was my favourite lipstick, Touch of Heaven, that I'd been looking for all week. I applied it with care and felt a bit better.

I could have killed Solly that morning as he lay in bed, cursing and moaning in between showers of self-pitying tears. He was now terrified of bumping into Borgy or his even more sadistic brother, who was known to hang out at the boxing club by Dockside. My coat was not mentioned, not once. I had plenty of flashbacks about the way it had been slashed while I was still wearing it and the rough way it was forced off my back. I went back to the kitchen and chopped some more carrots and tore up some Brussel tops like a maniac.

Then, at exactly 2.00 p.m. on the dot, Solly's mother and his Aunt Miriam arrived in a mini cab. "Oh, my Lord, look at you, my son," said his mother.

The pair of them were all over him like a rash but not one straight-forward question was addressed to him. The dinner was well received and eaten up, though Solly was not on top form, unsurprisingly. I could see that a couple of his front teeth had been chipped and one was loose. The apple pie and custard also went down well, leaving me with more than a full sink of washing up. Nobody offered to give me a hand and I thankfully left the three of them watching Fred Astaire and Ginger Rogers in one of their dancing musicals from the '40s on the television. The ladies had both brought some knitting with them and were happily clicking the needles until they dropped off to sleep and by the time I had finished the dishes and stacked the washing up, all three were in slumber with a backing soundtrack of snoring, sighing and Solly's moaning. I thought he looked pretty pasty – which made me decide to reapply some lipstick as, again, I needed to perk up myself. I desperately wanted to phone Joyce for some sympathy, support and advice but it was Sunday, a family day. The call would have to wait.

In my bedroom, I opened the biscuit tin again. It had originally contained a special Peek Freans' Assortment from a long-ago Christmas; there was Father Christmas tip-toeing into a peaceful bedroom with two angelic children fast asleep. It was a touching illustration that made me feel sad and resentful at the same time. I opened the tin and went through dried up make-up that shared space with some broken brooches, single earrings, that sort of thing. Wrapped up in some newspaper were a couple of items I had half-forgotten about and I slipped them into the deep pocket of my green cardigan.

I then crept silently into the sitting room as Fred and Ginger were tap dancing down a grand staircase. I felt in my pocket and selected the longer of the two hatpins. I carefully inserted into the corner of Solly's swollen and purple right eyelid and I held my breath and pushed it in just as far as it would go. I withdrew it and Solly shuddered slightly and took an inward sharp breath. It all felt like a dream, or a scene from a movie.

Ma and Miriam came to again at about 4.00 p.m. Solly remained on the sofa and looked quite a bad colour now. Ma got up slowly, bones creaking and popped her knitting back in her tapestry bag. She was about to telephone for a cab home when she suddenly gasped and her face went terribly red. "Alice, Solly's stopped breathing! Oh my Lord, have you got a mirror in your handbag?"

Silly question really, as I always have a little square mirror in my handbag; I use it when repairing lipstick or mascara when I am out and about. The mirror was snatched from me, a bit like my jacket was the evening before. Miriam held the mirror under Solly's chin and I noted that it was not steaming up.

"Call an ambulance, Alice!"

I wanted to say, "It looks a bit too late to me," but instead I dialled 999.

As I hung up, Ma started to shout again. "Call the coppers, Alice. That beating last night has done him in! They need to find that bleeding Borgy and nick him before he does a runner."

Soon the place was full of ambulance men and police officers and I nearly ran out of milk, making all those cups of tea. Quite a little gathering, as it turned out. Solly departed on his final journey to the local hospital mortuary and the police also disappeared with a blue light flashing towards Dockside, kindly dropping Ma and Miriam back home on the way.

Next morning, I phoned Joyce in her office and filled her in and thanked her too; she had been such a good advisor. I went upstairs in the afternoon, needing a little nap but I had just two more jobs to do first. Yesterday's cardigan was still on the bedroom chair. I emptied the pockets and put the cardigan into the laundry basket. Next, I re-wrapped the hatpins in the newspaper and replaced them in the biscuit tin, the entire contents of which I then decanted into a plastic bag, which I quickly threw down the rubbish chute on the balcony. I kept the tin though, as I had always liked it.

I settled down after a while and before I dropped off to sleep, I thought about a suitable hat for the funeral, although I knew I couldn't make any proper arrangements until I had taken the call from the coroner's office to release the body.

After a few weeks the inquest came back: the beating was deemed possibly a factor, but not conclusive. Borgy spent a few nights at Her Majesty's Pleasure in Brixton but was released due to the lack of evidence. The official line was that Solly's heart had just stopped after a very nice home-cooked lunch and during the film; no definite cause of death could be proved.

We picked a date for the funeral and I decided I would go without a hat and borrow a black silk scarf from Joyce instead.

The funeral will be next Thursday. On the Friday we might take a trip up west to see if I can find another leather coat; it won't be a black one either.

CONDEMNED

By Tony Ormerod

"The Lord is my shepherd; I shall not want."

The priest, plodding behind him, began to intone the well-known psalm; or was he a vicar? The man neither knew nor cared much now but, over the years, although not often, he had asked himself why men of the cloth felt compelled to deliver their contributions in such a downbeat, singsong and dreary fashion.

Hands strapped securely behind him and flanked by two burly warders; his planned final walk had begun.

Drowning people who managed to survive were reputed to see their lives flashing before them but, feeling remarkably calm, the man was concerned only for the present and the immediate future of which, as far as the law was concerned, little now remained. He had other ideas. Wanting to take his time, he was puzzled that the others were in such a hurry. After much thought he had told himself that a miracle would occur; the trap door would jam - it would refuse to do its job! Reading about that somewhere had convinced him that, inevitably, all would be well. His salvation depended on that rather than the more problematic alternative of the afterlife. However, in the murky and guilty depths of his mind there remained the niggling doubt of Divine intervention.

"Will it hurt?" he had enquired earlier of the two warders, who had shared a cell with him throughout the night and into the morning. Understandably avoiding eye contact, they offered the opinion that Albert was 'out of the top drawer' when it came to dispatching people. Both had considered the question comically ridiculous but then, having drawn the short straws, who were they to inflict additional anguish onto the prisoner?

"Yea though I walk through the valley of the shadow of death." That was technically correct but, excluding a final appearance at the Old Bailey when twelve incorruptible jurors had reached a unanimous conclusion, his life had been a lucky one. Surely that legendary good fortune would rescue him? He just managed to catch sight of Albert before the white hood was produced and utilised.

"And I will dwell in the house of the Lord forever."

The priest's "Amen" and the man's "Damn!" coincided.

WOUNDED IN ACTION

By Richard Miller

Private John Baxter, who was standing at one end of the trench, turned to his sergeant, David Callaghan and said: "Today's July 31st and you'd think it would be hot and sunny but no, it's pouring down and there's loads of mud in the trench."

"No pleasing some people," the sergeant replied.

Fifty yards away, one of the unit was speaking far too loudly. "Who's the noisy sod at the other end of trench, sergeant? I don't know him."

"Oh, he joined us the other day whilst you were in the hospital. Name is Bill Atkins. He's been coming out with a load of rubbish since he arrived. He said that he comes from your neck of the woods; I know you come from a small town so thought you might know him. He's been boasting about pinching someone else's fiancée and having affairs with married women - not the sort of thing you should you say when there are loads of men who haven't seen their womenfolk for ages. I'll introduce you later, assuming we get back in one piece! Anyway, great that you're back. We need good shots like you."

Baxter thought to himself, "I'd like to get my hands on him. Arrogant sod."

Callaghan looked at him. "I can see what you're thinking. Don't do anything silly. Tempting as it is."

At that, the company commander, Captain Henry Waters, strolled past and started bellowing out orders. "Right, lads, the artillery will be opening up in ten minutes and once there's enough smoke we'll be over the top. "

Captain Waters took up his post by Atkins. "Your first bit of action isn't it, Atkins? Hopefully not the last. I heard what you said about pinching someone else's fiancée. Any more talk like that and you'll be on a charge. The men's morale isn't good so hearing talk like that doesn't help. Will get you into trouble. Understand?"

"Yes, sir."

Waters walked back down the line knowing that for some this was their first action and they would be terrified. For those, he offered what words of comfort he could. For some, he offered encouragement and for one or two the captain's comments caused surprise.

Twenty minutes later, the captain gave the command to go over the top and into a land riddled with mud and holes and obstructed by fences. The sound of bullets and shells made hearing the commands from officers and NCOs almost impossible. Many of the soldiers screamed in fear or as they were hit by bullets; many old hands and young recruits alike would no longer see home.

*

Bill Atkins woke with a thumping headache and a sore jaw. Trying to look around, he discovered he couldn't see and was overcome with terror. "Help me!" he shouted. "I can't bloody see!"

He heard footsteps heading his way, the sound of feet on the duckboards that you found in trenches. Then he heard a female voice. "Keep calm...you're in a field hospital. We had to bandage your head as you were badly wounded two days ago. You did wake briefly yesterday but you were drowsy; all that morphine we gave you. I'll let the doctor know you're awake and he'll tell you the score. My guess is that you'll be shipped home. I'll be back in a few moments with the doctor."

"Private Atkins, I'm Doctor Lewis. Sorry to tell you but your head and especially your face has been badly wounded. I'm afraid to say that you've lost an eye, part of your jaw and a few teeth. We're shipping you off to Blighty - there's this new hospital in Sidcup, somewhere in Kent, and I've heard they are doing great work in repairing damaged faces. Some New Zealander, Harold Gillies, set up the hospital and he's supposed to be the best. Being where it is, hopefully the country air will do you the power of good. Beats being here in this hellhole."

"Thank you, sir."

With that, the doctor left and went over to the sister with instructions to make Atkins ready for the journey home.

The journey back from France was slow and painful. The boat and the trains were filled with the sounds of men crying out in agony and the soothing voices of the nursing staff. On arriving in London, the patients were sent in different directions. Atkins and a few others, along with a couple of nurses, were put on a train to Sidcup.

On the train one of the nurses was asked: "Why are we in a carriage by ourselves? Surely we're not the only passengers?"

"You're not. Sadly, some civilians can't cope with seeing injured soldiers. Bloody disgraceful if you ask me. Did they expect no one to be injured?"

As the train headed out to Kent, the scenery changed from built-up areas near Bermondsey to open country and farms.

At Sidcup, the patients were met by a couple of nurses. One of them introduced herself as Sister Walsh. "This is my colleague, Nurse Thomas. Our carriage is just around the corner. It's only about a twenty-minute ride to the hospital."

As they ascended, Bill and the others noted the oast houses near the station and the appropriately named pub, the Station Hotel. A couple of minutes after leaving the station Atkins noticed a number of women in work clothes coming out of a street called Manor Road. "Sister, where are those ladies heading to? The oast houses?"

"Oh, no, they are heading to Crayford to work in the Vickers factory. They live in a couple of houses in Manor Road. Requisitioned by the War Office, I believe. I wonder if they are fully aware of the damage and injuries caused by the munitions they make…"

As the carriage wound its way to the hospital a number of blue benches were visible. Anticipating the question, Nurse Thomas said: "Those benches are for the sole use of those at the hospital. Blue to match the colour of the uniforms you'll be given. We're hoping to open up a café in the High Street; somewhere for you lot to go and relax. Be warned, even though we've been here a while there are some locals who are still struggling to cope with you new arrivals and your injuries. Hopefully, in time, they'll be more welcoming."

The hospital was a large manor house and a number of huts, with the latter arranged in a star shape.

"All right, lads, we'll take you to the wards and later Dr. Gillies will come round for a chat. You'll like him. Bloody good at his job."

Atkins and the other newly arrived injured servicemen were taken to a ward and allocated beds. Looking around, they noticed men with bandages and what looked like elephant trunks joining their faces to their chests. Bill thought it was perhaps a strange experiment.

After ten minutes, the doors to the ward swung open and in strolled three doctors and a couple of matrons.

"Morning all. For those who don't know me, I'm Harold Gillies and as you can tell from my accent I'm not from this part of the world. For our new customers," there were chuckles from those who had been in the ward for some time, "it's my job and those of my colleagues here to re-build you. I can't say that it will be without pain and some of you may be here for some time but it's my view that you deserve to be given the best treatment. Henry Tonks, to my left here, is a doctor but also a bloody good artist and it's his job to paint your portraits. We use them for before and after treatment. Photographs will be taken but we find paintings more personal and detailed. To my right is Kelsey Fry. He's an excellent dentist and you'll be getting to see him close up."

*

Over the next few months Atkins had several operations to re-build his face. Although he would only have sight in one eye, and teeth which had been replaced with false ones, the hope was that his face would be almost as good as that he was born with. Bill learnt that the trunk-like tube was called a pedicle and transferred blood from a good part of the body to a damaged part. None of the operations were without pain but the morphine helped alleviate some of the discomfort.

As the months dragged by, the patients discussed military experiences, injuries, and their plans for the future, often with the gallows humour only found among those who have experienced pain and suffering.

"I wonder if I can become a model for a portrait artist after the war," said one brave wag. The comment was met with howls of laughter.

"Hoping to enter the shooting at the next Olympics, assuming that goes ahead. But with one eye, who knows?" said another.

The conversation flowed. Although it was occasionally grim, it had an undercurrent of optimism about it.

"I heard the other day about a bloke in another ward who was visited by his fiancée. When she took a look at him, she broke off the engagement. Came with a friend who was bloody annoyed when that happened."

"Gillies is trying to get us jobs and has set up a workshop to help us learn a trade. Even heard that a football team is to be set up. Hope he gets some recognition for all this; the man is a genius."

"You remember Robert Scott, who died on the way back from reaching the South Pole in 1912? His widow, Kathleen works here."

"The nurses here are lovely. I wonder what my chances are…?"

*

One sunny morning in early March, Atkins was sitting in the ward browsing through one of the many magazines in the hospital. He was reading the latest about the war in Europe when a nurse entered the ward. "Bill, there is a visitor for you. He's in the main building."

He rose and walked over. On entering, he saw his former commanding officer, Henry Waters. "Morning, Private Atkins. I'm in England on leave so thought I'd pop over and see how you're getting on. Important to keep an eye on the rank and file. Those injuries you suffered were horrific. Good to see you looking better. I've heard great things about this place."

"Morning, sir. Thank you, sir, for visiting. I see you've been promoted to the rank of major. Congratulations."

"Shall we go for a walk? You can tell me how you're getting on and all about this place."

"Well, as you can see, sir, there are a number of huts for us to recuperate in and where we wait for treatment. The main house is for the doctors and the operations. The staff here, especially Doctor Gillies, are brilliant. The nurses are smashing as well - if you get my drift, sir."

"I do, Private. Remember our conversation before we 'went over'?"

"Yes, sir. I haven't tried to pinch the wife or girlfriend of one of my fellow patients. These guys have suffered enough without me adding to their woes."

"Excellent to hear, Atkins. Anyway, let's get down to business and the real reason for my visit. I would have come earlier but with the fighting and the problems with tracking you down..."

Atkins muttered: "Oh? I'm intrigued, sir."

"On that day when we went over, I heard Private Baxter and Sergeant Callaghan talking about your philandering in your home village. I suspect Baxter was unhappy, and damned angry, as he thought you were having an affair with his wife... That may well have been the case but..." He paused. "I also know you were seeing mine." He was silent for a moment as he let the revelation sink in. "I hoped that I'd killed you on the first day of the Third Battle of Ypres but with all the confusion and smoke it wasn't to be. I even thought that Baxter might kill you, given what I said to him. Everyone thought it was German bullets that injured you. But," he shrugged, "one bullet is pretty much like another in the heat of battle. So..." he lowered his voice, "I'm here to finish the job."

Strangely, Atkins seemed almost unperturbed. "And how do you expect to get away with it, sir? The regiment will be looking for you. The staff here know I've a visitor and once they realise I've disappeared, will call the police."

"True," said Waters. "But I'm on leave and once I've finished with you, I'll be heading overseas. Somewhere the authorities will never find me. There's absolutely no point in trying to run away. There's no doubt that I'm a lot fitter than you." He laughed as he looked at Atkins. "Did you honestly think that you would get away with having an affair with my wife?" Waters was calm, with a self-assuredness that at last made the private realise the danger he was in.

Waters pulled out a gun.

Atkins leapt at the major and the two of them struggled with each other.

A shot rang out.

A body fell to the ground.

After a few seconds the survivor of the struggle started to run… but he wouldn't get far.

HUSH MONEY

By Richie Stress

It was late in the day when he awoke in his own bed. Daniel embraced the demagogic twilight until it drifted into the ether and the hard slap of reality dropped itself like a doodlebug on a doll's house.

He checked his phone – one single message from an unknown number. It was her.

*

His memories of the previous night were somewhat hazy: a club, a girl, a taxi back to hers. And then he had awoken in her bed. The main light was on, blinding him.

Everything in the room was pink. Girly and fluffy was how he would have described it. There were framed pictures of horses dotted around the walls. Last night's fling was lying on her back, snoring sweetly beside him, her pillow stained with the thick makeup yet to be removed.

He had a banging headache; probably from dehydration, he thought. That and the copious amounts of Strongbow cider he had consumed. He glanced over at the table next to the bed for something to ease the pain. There was nothing except for a passport. Instinctively, he opened it and grinned at the mugshot. It was unmistakably her in the monochrome photograph, but with her hair plain and she wore no makeup.

He scanned the profile. Dora Wendy Hush – so now he knew her name. Date of birth – *shit, that can't be right*. He sat up and took a closer look, trying to clear his head as he studied the figures. He counted the years out on his fingers.

'Turn the light out,' the girl mumbled sleepily and turned her head away with a gentle sigh.

*

The church was the same as he had remembered it. The same wooden décor, naked brick walls and cold hollow interior. Flames flickered from the odd solitary candle.

He sat at the end of a pew, staring into space as a heavy bang from the confessional door echoed soullessly around the building. It made him jump and he felt embarrassed, although a quick scan confirmed there were no witnesses.

He sighed.

A woman emerged from the booth. She looked old to Daniel, who was twenty-one, although she might have been middle-aged and sickly; it was hard to tell in that light. She used a cheap metal walking frame to shuffle out, her head lowered in concentration.

Daniel felt uncomfortable. He did not know whether to help or if she would find such a gesture patronising. Finally, she looked up and grinned at him in an "*isn't life a bitch but you have to laugh, don't you?*" kind of a way and headed for the exit.

Daniel looked back at the nameplate on the door. "Fr. Seamus" was inscribed on a dirty silver plaque. He waited until "walking-frame woman" was out of sight before venturing into the minuscule room.

'Bless me, Father, for I have sinned.' Daniel knelt on the tiny step. 'It's been many years since my last confession.'

'Go on, my son,' came a craggy Irish accent from beyond the curtain.

'Well, you see, I met this girl last night and we went back to her place; well, I mean, I thought it was her place. And anyway, you know what happens in this sort of situation and then I left and went home, but...'

'And did you have relations with this person?' the priest interrupted.

'Yes, Father.'

'And now you're afraid she may become pregnant, is that it?'

'No, we used precautions. The thing is, afterwards we both passed out and when I woke up I found her passport and she's only 15 years old, Father.'

There was a short pause. 'So, you feel guilty because you forced yourself on her, is that it?'

'What? No, it was consensual. What am I going to do, Father? Please help me.'

*

Of course, the sheets would need washing; so would the makeup-sodden pillowcase.

Several streets away, Daniel's fling was tidying away all evidence of the night before. Her family were due back early the following morning and she had to make sure everything was as it should be.

She placed another empty can of Strongbow into a carrier bag. On one previous occasion, she had spent the money her parents had provided for a takeaway meal to purchase booze. She'd thought she got away with it until her folks had checked the waste bins outside the house. Instead of pizza boxes, her mother had found empty lager cans. This time she would dispense the contents at a bottle bank on the other side of town and rescue some cardboard left outside the local KFC and place it outside with the other rubbish.

She noticed the passport lying open on the bedside table and guessed that her plan had worked. She placed it carefully inside the drawer and rummaged through the plastic bag before finally finding her prize. Gleefully, she studied the smelly contents of the sad-looking, slimy rubber sheath and grinned.

*

Daniel took another swig from his bottle of Amstel. He was feeling a whole lot better.

He scanned the view from his luxury suburban apartment. The sun was setting on another hot and cloudless day. Life as a highly specialised freelance I.T. consultant was proving to be a pretty cushy number. He was his own boss and only worked if he needed to; considering the going rate for his particular area of expertise was pretty much off the chart these days, an hour or two a day was proving to be more than enough to get by on – and then some.

He made a silent toast to Father Seamus. The priest had given him a brief lecture on various conjugal decrees involving rabbis in the Mishnah, betrothal being more important than intercourse and Our Lady being Dora's age when she gave birth to Our Lord. He had not really understood much of it but was relieved to find the priest was pretty impervious to his situation.

He had given Daniel some prayers to say and sent him on his way, having instructed him it was probably best all round if

Daniel break off all contact with this particular girl. 'Best stick to those of your own age,' were his final words of wisdom.

And that was all it took to relieve the mind-crushing guilt. After all, if Father Seamus had a hotline to God and the man upstairs was cool with everything then who was he to argue? Daniel raised his glass to good old Roman Catholic forgiveness.

*

'Look, something's happened – I need you to get over here right now and help me,' Dora said. It had been nearly three weeks since their meeting. Daniel cursed himself for not blocking her number after his brief farewell text message. She was talking at such a speed he could barely make out the words.

Dora, I told you not to contact me and I told you the reason.'

'I know, but there's no one else I can ask.'

'Dora, I shouldn't even be talking to you.'

'If you don't come and help me right now, I'll tell someone and say you made me. I kept the condom and it's got your evidence on it. I swear; please just do this one simple thing and you'll never see me ever again, I promise.'

'What about your parents?'

'They're away until next week. Come quick.'

*

Daniel parked his black BMW and made his way along the road towards the end of the cul-de-sac where Dora lived.

She was waiting by the open door. Her eyes were red, cheeks mascara-stained. Then, without a single word, she was bounding the steep stairs – the same stairs Daniel remembered from their previous encounter. A worn-out green and brown carpet led him upwards.

He followed her to what he guessed must be the same room from before. This time he noticed the words "Dora's Room" written in colourful sparkly letters, surrounded by several cartoony unicorns. She flung open the door and pulled him inside.

There was a pale figure lying supine on the bed. He was shaven-headed, small and skinny, displaying needle tracks on both arms. Daniel guessed he was probably between 16 and 18

59

years old. He had deep ligature marks around his neck, wrist and ankles.

He was not breathing.

Dora was saying something, screaming at Daniel. He heard the word "accident" mentioned at least once. He felt nauseous; a strange dizziness threatened to engulf him. He crouched onto his haunches.

'What the fuck!' was all he could say.

Dora kept moving frenetically from one side of the room to the other, her arms flailing wildly. 'Jesus, Dora.' Daniel stood up and grabbed her by the elbows.

'He wanted me to do it,' she said, sobbing violently, her whole body shaking. 'I got carried away in the moment. I didn't mean it, I swear I didn't.'

Daniel guided Dora to a chair and knelt in front of her. He loosened the grip on her arms. 'Dora, listen to me, this is serious. We've got to tell the authorities and we have to do it now, do you understand?' He looked toward the lifeless figure on the bed.

'No way, no way!' Dora sobbed loudly. Her phone started ringing. Glancing at the screen, she instantly regained her composure before answering. 'Hi, Mum. Yeh, everything's fine here. Yeh, you know, just stayed in and watched *Britain's Got Talent*, mainly. Yeh, Simon Cowell is an annoying twat. Ok, see you Friday. Love you, bye. Bye-bye.'

*

It was not at all easy, trying to drag what was literally a dead weight off a bed, manoeuvre it out of the room at an angle and forwards towards the top of the Hush family staircase and, as Dora could not bear to touch any part of the corpse, it was left to Daniel to cram the body into her Disney-themed duvet cover before the two-person operation could start.

Dora sat behind the bundle at the top of the stairs and began to brace herself.

'What are you doing?' Daniel said.

'Slide him down, innit,' Dora replied.

'Seems a bit callous though,' Daniel said.

She glared at him before thrusting out her feet. *Frozen's* Elsa and Kristoff rolled over and over before the whole thing clomped lifelessly to the bottom of the stairs.

A full minute passed.

'What was his name?' Daniel asked.

'Jim,' Dora said.

'Is that your dog scratching to be let out?' said Daniel.

Dora looked at him. 'I don't have a dog.'

Suddenly, the duvet was moving. Dora got to her feet.

'Don't panic. It's the rigor mortis setting in; it's what happens after – you know,' Daniel said.

A muffled yelp confirmed that this probably was not the rigor mortis setting in as the bundle began a desperate and frenetic dance along the hallway. In the blink of an eye, Dora was at the bottom of the stairs, helping to remove a somewhat disorientated Jim from his bondage of cartoon linen.

Jim stared up the stairs and covered his nakedness as his pale cheeks morphed into the colour of rhubarb. Daniel had never seen anyone look so thoroughly pathetic.

*

Stirring his tea, Daniel stared forlornly out of the window. He glanced down at the green herbal infusion string hanging limply by the side of his brown paper cup.

This was the third time in as many weeks she had been late for their meet-up and each one made him feel increasingly antsy.

It had been over a month since the "Jim Incident" and Dora's promises to stay out of Daniel's life had proved, predictably, null and void.

He glanced around – no one he recognised from their previous trysts. That was something, at least.

Every week she had arrived later than the one before. As of now, she was a full hour and forty-five minutes overdue. He felt his bladder start to complain. He got to his feet; at least a toilet trip would relieve the boredom for several moments if nothing else.

'Going somewhere?' said a voice. So she was here. She had a cluster of shopping. She sat down opposite him. 'Not thinking of standing me up, I hope?'

'You're late again,' Daniel said.

'Am I?' Dora was arranging the various bags of goodies underneath their table. 'I had some things to do. Got some great stuff – nothing for you though, sorry.'

A waitress hovered into view. 'Anything I can get for you?'

Dora proceeded to order herself the most spectacular coffee on the menu, some walnut cake, a chocolate donut and a family size bag of cheese and onion crisps. She looked over at Daniel. 'Anything you want?'

Daniel shook his head and waited until the waitress was well out of earshot. 'Why do you have to order so much? These meetings are supposed to be brief. That's what we agreed on,' he said.

'Chill out, Danny boy. Don't forget I'm eating for two now.' Dora patted her stomach. 'Not showing yet though.'

'Keep your voice down,' Daniel said.

'Why? There's no one here who gives a shit.'

Daniel took a sip of tea. 'So how is the father to be? Still breathing, is he?'

'Oh, Jim's fine. Assuming he is the father, of course.' She threw him a sly wink and continued, 'Been really supportive actually. Said he's gonna come with me to the clinic for the – you know, the procedure.'

Good old Jim, Daniel thought. You could always rely on a sixteen-year-old smackhead to do the right thing.

The waitress brought over Dora's order and shuffled back towards the kitchen. Daniel tried to change the subject. 'I thought you were supposed to be back in school by now?'

'Who needs school when they've got a regular income?' shrugged Dora, sipping from the huge coffee mug.

'Yes – my bloody income! You're supposed to be saving towards the…'

'The abortion,' Dora mumbled through a mouthful of cake. 'Ok! Time to hand it over, mate.'

'But you're bleeding me dry!' said Daniel.

'Not my problem,' Dora replied.

Daniel passed her a brown paper envelope under the table and stood up to leave.

'Sit down!' she ordered.

'But I need the loo,' said Daniel.

'Sit down now or I'll cause a scene.'

Half an hour of uncomfortable silence followed until Dora finally gathered her belongings and left a squirming Daniel to pay the bill.

*

The next day, Daniel decided he needed a walk to clear his head. Following several hours of deliberation, he finally settled on a leisurely stroll around Skullingstone Park, just a short drive away. Having parked and paid and displayed his ticket, he set off along a hilly track towards the wooded area that surrounded a privately maintained golf course.

It was a sunny day with some light cloud. Being an early afternoon on a Wednesday, there were not too many people to get in his way: a couple of mums with prams and the obligatory dog walkers were about as much as he would contend with.

On reaching the apex of the track he stopped and turned to admire the view. He took a swig from his water bottle and sighed. He needed to come up with a plan – a way to get himself out of this unfortunate mess. Surely he was clever enough to outsmart a 15-year-old mother-to-be and her junky boyfriend.

Maybe his best course of action would be simply to confess; throw himself on the mercy of the powers that be and claim ignorance? The only problem there was it would end up being Dora's word against his. If he had learnt one thing, she had a talent for manipulating people until she got her own way.

Even if he did confess, it would be only a matter of time before word got around. He would then lose his blossoming career as well as his reputation – his life would be ruined.

The alternative, however, was to continue to pay Dora off. In his heart, he knew her demands were likely to increase over time – plus she had a loser boyfriend who was funding a drug habit. She would eventually bleed him dry and blow his cover anyway.

He could kill her, of course, but he was not the killing type and he knew it. The guilt alone would gradually destroy his fragile psyche.

Ok, so the only evidence was the used condom she claimed to have rescued following their night of passion. What if she was lying about that? It might be worth calling her bluff, but was it worth the risk? On the other hand, it was the only real evidence that anything had ever taken place.

If he could somehow get his hands on said prophylactic and destroy it, the rest of her case would become circumstantial. It could be enough to put him in the clear.

Great! So now he had a plan. It was time to turn detective on her arse. If Dora wanted to go to war with him, bring it on. The only problem of course was how to get his hands on the condom, presumably hidden away somewhere at her parents' house.

*

Tracking down Dora's smackhead boyfriend had not been the easiest of missions. Even being the computer genius he was, the fact that Daniel did not know Jim's last name meant he had nothing to go on. He could not search the electoral roll for an address – that was if, in fact, Jim even had one – and he could not exactly ask Dora without arousing suspicion. He would have to do this the old-fashioned way.

Following the latest cash drop off at the coffee shop he found himself hot on Dora's tail. Through a mouthful of cake, she had let it slip she was on her way to meet Jim, who needed to borrow some petty cash to pay off a debt.

This was the opportunity Daniel had been waiting for. Dora would lead him to Jim, whereupon he would stalk the pair until she was out of the picture. Daniel would offer the junky a deal. Jim would then find the condom and hand it over to Daniel for a generous cash reward. What could possibly go wrong?

From his seat in the coffee shop, Daniel watched nonchalantly as Dora made her way along the high street, crossed the road and took a left. As soon as she was out of sight Daniel hot-footed it after her. He reached the turning and made his way around, keeping himself out of sight as much as possible. In the distance, he could just make out her ample backside as she turned onto an adjacent footpath.

Daniel knew there were only two exits from there. Either she was going to enter a housing estate – if this was the case then the chase was as good as over – or she was headed for the local swing park. He ran for 200 metres and stopped by the entrance of the footpath. There was no sign of her. Breathing heavily, he jogged clumsily towards the opening that led to the swing park.

She was sitting on a bench barely 15 yards away. He ducked out of sight between a graffiti-covered fence and a large metal post, praying she had not seen him. He could spy on her safely from here.

Dora was sitting next to someone and from what he could make out they seemed to be having some kind of heated discussion. Unfortunately, he was slightly too far away to hear what was being said. Daniel assumed the other person must be Jim and the argument was about the money she had promised him.

On closer inspection, he discovered the conversation was with another girl. Not only that, but another girl who looked so similar to Dora that they could be sisters. She was wearing different clothes and her hair was slightly different, but the resemblance was remarkable. In fact, they could easily be identical twins. Dora had mentioned she had an older sister who enjoyed holidaying with their parents, but to look this much alike was astonishing.

The argument seemed to be getting more intense as the sisters screamed and shouted at each other. Suddenly, Dora grabbed her sibling by the hair and threw her to the ground. In the process, the other girl's phone fell onto the concrete. Dora stamped on the phone spitefully with her heel and hurried away, screaming, 'Stay away from him, Dora!'

Daniel knew he should pursue his quarry but something was puzzling him. Why had Dora called her sister by her own name? Surely they didn't have the same name, did they? It would be hard enough to tell them apart as it was. How lazy must their parents be to have given twin daughters exactly the same name?

Seeing that *his* Dora was by now long gone, he made his way towards the *other new* Dora. She was trying to get to her feet and it was causing her some discomfort.

'Are you ok there?' said Daniel.

'Leave me alone,' came the reply.

Daniel picked up the broken phone and offered it to her. She snatched it away from him. Tears were running down her cheeks.

He tried again. Look, I know your sister and I was just wondering why she called you Dora.'

The girl stared at him suspiciously. 'Because that's my name, stupid.' She sat down, shaking, as Daniel perched timidly on the arm of the bench.

'But you're her sister, right?'

'Yeh, so?'

Daniel sighed. 'So, you are twins and you're both named Dora?'

'What? No, I'm Dora and she's Mandy and we ain't twins. I thought you said you were a mate of hers?' She tutted.

Goosebumps erupted over Daniel's skin. 'So, hang on a minute, if you're not twins then how old is Mandy?'

'Why are you asking all these questions – are you police?'

'Do I look like police?'

She studied him closely. 'Yeh, alright then, but what you asking for?'

Daniel spent the next ten minutes relating the whole sorry saga. He told her about the passport, the Jim incident, the proposed abortion and how she had been blackmailing him for hush money.

The *real* Dora looked at him in utter bemusement. 'Oh my god, she told you all that? It's all lies. Jim aint even her boyfriend. She keeps trying to steal him away from me by buying his drugs for him. I can't believe she's been using my room as some kind of knocking shop too!'

'Dora, please – just tell me how old she is?'

'No need to panic, lover boy, ok – she's 19, nearly 20.'

'And is she pregnant?'

'Err, no.'

Daniel felt a modicum of weight lift from his shoulders. 'So was that what the two of you were arguing about? Jim the junky?'

'Don't call him that. James promised me he's gonna try and give up the smack and then marry me. He knows I'm saving myself for 'im.'

'Ok, well best of luck with that then.' Daniel said

'I don't think I like you very much as it goes,' Dora replied.

'Look, Dora, do you wanna go grab a drink so we can discuss this further? My treat,' Daniel offered.

Dora turned to leave. 'Get lost, freak!'

*

Daniel sat stirring his empty cup with a wooden spatula. A waitress he recognised smiled at him warmly. The girl he now knew to be Mandy breezed in, laden down with her latest bag of goodies.

'Hey Danny, get me the usual, will ya?' Daniel stared silently as she plonked herself onto the seat. 'Well, go on then, I haven't got all day,' she said.

Daniel continued to hold her gaze until he finally had her full attention. 'So how are we today then, *Mandy Hush*?'

He remembered that expression in her eyes – it was the same look of terror she exhibited when she thought Jim was dead.

Slowly, the mask of nonchalance returned and she smirked. 'So you know. Took you long enough. So what – it don't change nothing.'

Daniel gritted his teeth hard. 'It changes everything! I know how old you are so you can cut out the paedophile crap – you're evil, Mandy, you know that.'

'That's no way to talk to the mother of your unborn child.'

'Stop lying to me. You're not even pregnant!' Daniel got to his feet as if to leave.

'Don't go! I'm sorry. We can come to an arrangement.' Mandy's eyes filled with tears. 'If I don't get Jim's drugs for im then he's gonna leave me and I'll have no one to help me with the baby.' Daniel pushed past her and headed for the door. She ran and grabbed his arm. 'You go out that door and I'll make you regret it.'

Daniel pushed her away. 'Have a nice life, Mandy.' He turned away and walked out of the coffee shop towards the bustling high street.

*

Jim Duran had been hearing rumours. Usually this didn't bother him too much as he didn't really care what people thought about him – i.e., that he was a garbage-head loser. As long as he could get high and have his needs met regularly then life was sweet. However, it seemed the news of his near-death experience had got around and the circumstances of it were becoming ever more fanciful. So much, in fact, that he was being pretty much snubbed by everyone he knew.

There were various accounts of the night's events. They included one of him enjoying a threesome with Mandy and some guy; another where he had asked to be dressed up like Anna from *Frozen*; and his favourite, where he had apparently tried to persuade Mandy to join him in a suicide pact.

He knew most of the stories were the product of Mandy's twisted imagination. He also knew this was some kind of payback for liking her younger sister, who he did actually have a genuine fondness for. He knew it drove Mandy crazy. She could provide him with the kinkiest of sexual fantasies as well as money for heroin, but she could never experience the deeper loving connection he had with Dora.

He would speak to Mandy and get her to retract all her spiteful claims. It was time he left her and her scheming ways, once and for all. He determined to raise his game by spending some quality time with Dora – the one person who had ever shown him any genuine support throughout his short life.

*

Across town, Dora and Mandy were watching *Love Island* on TV.

'See you got some more new tops,' Dora said.

'Yep, and no, you can't have a lend,' Mandy said.

'Where d'you get the cash for those then?' Dora said.

'None of your business.' Mandy tucked herself into the sofa and concentrated on the screen. 'He's buff. I wouldn't mind a go on that.'

'You're such a slag, Mandy. Why can't you let me have James when you've got plenty of your own? I'm surprised you ain't pregnant, the way you carry on.'

'Yeh, but I do a damn good impression of someone who is.' Mandy laughed and turned her attention away from the television to face her sister. 'I got a nice bit of cash flow from some mug who thought I needed an abortion. You better not tell anyone, Dora, or I'll tell Mum and Dad about what you get up to with Jim Duran.'

68

'I don't get up to anything with James. I told you, I'm saving myself.' Mandy glared at her, disbelievingly. Dora continued, 'So this guy's been helping you out then?'

'Well, he was, but he called my bluff so I've run outta leverage.'

'Well, create some new leverage then. Say that if he don't cough up, you'll cry rape or something like that,' Dora urged.

'My word against his though, innit.'

'Not if you've got a witness to back you up, right? I do this and you let me have James – for good this time.'

Mandy pursed her lips, then raised her eyebrows in confirmation of their agreement.

*

'Your name is Daniel Rarebird, is that correct?' The police officer seated opposite leaned back in his chair. Daniel watched as the reels on a tape recorder began circling.

'Yes,' Daniel said.

'So, you went back to Mandy's parents' house?' asked the officer.

'That's correct.'

'And how much had you been drinking, roughly?'

'I think about three pints.'

'But you can't be sure?'

'No, but…'

'What happened then?'

'We went upstairs and… had sex.'

'She claims you tied her up and raped her.'

'That's not what happened.'

'You just said you can't remember how much you drank that night so how do you know that's not what happened?'

Daniel was firm about it. 'I didn't rape her!'

The policeman rocked forward on his chair. 'Daniel, why would somebody keep hold of a used condom? It seems like a strange thing to do, don't you think?' Daniel shrugged. The officer continued. 'Maybe because something terrible had happened to that person and they needed to keep some evidence of what had taken place?'

After several hours of similar questioning, Daniel had admitted to nothing and was allowed to leave the station. He determined that Mandy was not going to beat him. Besides, he was an upstanding member of the community with an amazing apartment and brilliant career, whereas she was an untrustworthy, unemployed sleep-around still living at home. How could they take her word against his? At last he had called her bluff and she had nothing on him. Finally, he was winning.

Several miles away, Dora wiped the fog from the cracked screen of her Nokia phone and made a call that would change his life forever.

*

The courtroom felt wooden and soulless. Nearly two years had passed since Daniel had last set eyes on Mandy. He stared at her across the room but she avoided eye contact. The jury was ushered in and took their places. Everyone stood as the judge entered and told them to be seated.

'Will the defendant please rise,' the judge said, gesturing towards the court clerk.

'Will the forewoman of the jury please stand,' said the clerk, as an ashen-faced woman stood nervously to attention. The clerk continued, 'Have you reached a verdict upon which you are all agreed? Please answer yes or no.'

'Yes,' said the forewoman.

'On the count of blackmail, what is your verdict?'

'Guilty.'

'And on the account of false accusation, what is your verdict?'

'Guilty.'

In the public gallery, Daniel pumped his fist in the air. Dora let out a cry of joy and threw her arms around him in celebration.

The judge called for silence. 'Mandy Louise Hush, you have been found guilty on all charges.'

*

Outside the courthouse, Jim was failing to rock two-month-old baby Elsa to sleep in her pram. A short time later he was joined by Dora and Daniel. They were beaming at one another in triumph.

70

'I guess it went well then?' Jim said.

'I can't believe she got six years. I guess that means we'll all be safe for a while anyway,' Dora said.

'If it hadn't been for your testimony – getting her entire confession on tape like that – it could have been me up there instead,' Daniel said.

'At least now we can bring up the brat without having to look over our shoulders all the time,' Jim said.

'Who are you calling a brat, James Duran?' Dora joked.

Jim turned and shook Daniel forcefully by the hand. 'I never officially thanked you for getting me into The Priory and helping me get off the gear.'

'Why don't I just take it out of your wages for the next five years? Besides, I needed someone I could trust to help me expand RareBird Industries,' Daniel said.

'So, you immediately thought: "I know; I'll employ a no-skills junkie still in rehab. Oh yeh, and I'll also let him and his 17-year-old recently pregnant girlfriend move in too." Now what could possibly go wrong there?' Jim said, smiling.

'Worked though, didn't it?' Daniel said. 'Plus there's always strength in numbers when randy Mandy's on the prowl.'

They all laughed. Dora reached inside the pram, held Elsa aloft and sniffed. 'I think the "brat" might need changing. James, could you do the honours please?'

She handed the baby over. Dora and Daniel watched Jim wrinkle his nose as he disappeared up the steps towards the courthouse facilities, holding Elsa.

'Do you think we should tell him?' Dora said.

'No, absolutely not. It will break his heart; he'll go straight back on the smack.'

I wish I'd never done that stupid D.N.A. test thingy, but I had to know if Elsa was your daughter or James'. It was doing my head in,' Dora said.

Daniel sighed. 'I know it was.' He put his arm around Dora, kissed her tenderly on the head and kept a concentrated gaze upon the concrete courthouse steps.

PURPLE HAZE

By A.J.R. Kinchington

She scraped the lilac dye from under her fingernails and glanced at Si lying prone on the sofa. Distaste at the sight of him narrowed her eyes and reinforced her determination to be rid of him.

*

He opened one eye and then the other. Light pierced his retina and sent searing pain up into his skull.

'Christ,' he spluttered, shutting both eyes tightly. He gripped the arms of the chair and slowly sat up, his fingers feeling the cigarette burns in the leather. Cautiously, he half opened his eyes. Nothing appeared to be burning other than the two-bar electric fire. The right leg of his jeans felt uncomfortably hot and he realised he had been asleep and dangerously close to receiving a severe burn. The small clock on the side table showed it was two-thirty in the afternoon. Rising, he kicked over the glass containing the remains of his whisky and watched as it formed a small, dark patch on the already stained rug. Stepping over it, he made his way into the kitchen. There it sat, winking at him with all the *come and get me* of an alluring female. He smiled at the thought and, as his jaw ached, immediately regretted it. Resisting the bottle of golden charm, he went to the bathroom and showered, but left his two-day beard alone. Running his hand over his dark, wet hair he spied himself in the mirror. A large bruise on his jawline was turning purple. Half smiling, he said out loud: 'Come on, Lewis, maybe this is your lucky day.' Returning dressed to the living area, he flicked on the TV.

Francesca Cumani was announcing that the 2018 Gold Cup horses and riders were in position and Might Bite was the favourite to win. The field was big, thirty-five horses, and soon the favourite was leading, but his horse Native River was neck and neck with it. The last of the fences came into view and he stood up, urging his horse on. 'Come on, Dicky!' he shouted as his horse came home first past the post. Today, Richard Johnson was his saviour. 'You beauty, I knew it was my lucky day!' Lewis yelled.

A knock at the door broke his elation. The young girl from across the hall stood there. 'Have you got a spare ciggy?'

'No. No money either.' Lewis closed the door. Since he had moved into this flat six months ago, she had been a constant beggar at his door. He wished he had not given her money the first three times but, with her pale face, bright lilac dreadlocks and kohl-etched eyes, she had looked so fragile.

He was a push-over for a sob story, but he was barely able to support himself; his redundancy money was fast disappearing.

Picking up his jacket, keys and the all-important betting slip, he headed for the door. The sound of her boots on the stairs made him hesitate. The downstairs fire door slammed shut and he continued. The door to her flat was slightly open, the lock hanging off. He remembered two nights ago hearing shouting, swearing and banging. He had ignored it as the flats had all sorts of people coming and going at all hours and he didn't want to get involved. But he was curious about her.

Outside, he walked the twenty minutes to the bookies, collected his winnings, picked up the Racing Post, bypassed the Yacht pub and headed for the café. He sat at his usual table by the window and before his order arrived downed two painkillers and opened the racing pages. The café began to fill up with kids from school. They jostled each other for seats whilst talking loudly and laughing. His friends these days were William Hill and Johnnie Walker, who asked no questions and accepted him unreservedly.

When he got home, satisfied with his day (for his expectations were limited), the TV was still on. Pouring the last of the amber nectar into his glass, he wondered what life had in store for him. He didn't have long to wait. There was an insistent knocking at his door. The girl from across the landing was standing there, shaking and crying, black rivers of mascara running into her small cleavage. 'Come quickly, I think he's dead.'

'Who is?'

'He won't wake up. He won't wake up. Si.'

He grabbed his keys, mobile and hurried after her.

73

Si was motionless, sprawled out on the sofa, his face pale, traces of blood at his mouth. He felt for a pulse; there was none. She was pacing up and down, whispering something inaudible.

A needle was on a side table, along with various small plastic bags containing tablets.

He looked at her, then at the table. A question hung in the air. 'I'll call an ambulance and wait with you,' he said.

Fifteen minutes later two paramedics arrived. They examined Si and asked what his name was and what had happened. 'Simon Baldwin,' she said. 'He was like this when I got home.'

One of them advised her to sit down and explained that there was nothing they could do and that the police had to come. She was shivering and clearly distressed.

When two policemen arrived, they spoke to the medics, who were asked to wait until a doctor came.

Then the questions started. 'Your name, Miss?'

'Verity Blasé.'

Nodding towards Si, the officer asked, 'Is he your boyfriend?'

'No. Just a friend. He's been here for three weeks. He's been sofa surfing.'

'Do you know any of his family?'

'No, I think they kicked him out.'

The officer looked at the canvases on the walls. Mostly they were garish depictions of gothic scenes, blacks and purples that matched her appearance. 'This your flat?' It was more a statement than a question.

She nodded.

'Does Simon have a mobile?'

She shook her head. 'He said he lost it.'

'Do you know anyone we can call, maybe other friends?'

'His friend Duncan works at the Yacht pub down the road.'

The police officer turned to Lewis. 'And you are?'

'Lewis Archer. I'm a neighbour, across the landing. She asked me to help, that's all.'

Two female officers and a doctor appeared.

Lewis was not happy. Coming to help was one thing, but this scenario was causing him acute anxiety. He needed to leave, now. 'Can I go now?' he asked.

'Yes, but we have a few more questions. Perhaps Verity and an officer can go to your flat until we finish here?'

Reluctantly, Lewis nodded his head.

*

Verity was curled up in his chair. The officer introduced herself as Sue and said she wanted to hear a bit more about them both. Lewis went to his kitchen. He really needed a drink but thought better of it. He needed a clear head if questions were to be answered.

Between tears, Verity told Sue that Simon was a fellow student at St. Martin's Art School. He was a talented artist but had been using drugs and was having problems at home. She had offered to let him stay for a few days, but his moods had swung from high to very low. He was eighteen. She didn't know much else about him as he had been evasive about his past. Today she had left at about three o'clock to go to the library as she didn't have Wi-Fi. She thought Si would sleep off what he had taken. She had come home around four-thirty and found him unresponsive.

Sue asked her if there was a family member that could come to be with her.

Verity said her family were all in New Zealand. Two years ago, when she was eighteen, she had come to study in London. She had friends from art school and usually hung out with them.

At this point they heard loud activity from across the landing: footsteps echoing down the three flights of stairs and voices in hushed tones. There was a knock at the door and one of the officers came in. 'We've spoken to Duncan at the pub, and Simon's family are going to the police station at Bexleyheath. We will get more information then. Verity, Sue will take you back to your flat.' He turned to Lewis. 'A few answers from you may help.'

Lewis gave an account of himself and his day. He was twenty-four; he'd been in the flat for six months; he was unemployed, and kept himself to himself. Today he had been to the bookies at three o'clock and then to the café. It could all be verified.

'So, what happened?' the officer asked, nodding at the now purple and yellow bruising on Lewis' face.

75

'Had a bit too much to drink. Had a fall.' He would later tell the same lie to Verity.

Neither Lewis nor Verity elaborated on their answers. Facts were easy.

*

Three days later Lewis answered his door. Verity stood there; her transformed appearance startled him. Her face was devoid of make-up and her lilac hair was swept up in a high ponytail. She had abandoned her heavy black boots and wore a soft white dress that exposed her arms. A tattoo of the word "Truth" entwined with large red roses went from shoulder to wrist. Without her Alice Cooper eyes and curtain of hair she was beautiful. Lewis felt something happen to his chest.

'Can I come in?'

'Sure.'

She went to his chair, curled up and offered a hesitant smile.

'Any news?' Lewis asked.

'I'm being charged with possession. The inquest on Si may be six weeks or more.'

'Possession?'

'Well, they found more coke stashed away, but at £80 I don't know how Si could afford it. He said he was skint, and I guess I now know why. But the gear was found in my flat. I don't do drugs; alcohol has been my thing.'

There didn't seem much more to say so Lewis went to get his whisky and gestured to her.

'No thanks, I can't.' He raised an eyebrow. 'I'm on eight of the twelve steps. I'm afraid I might topple off.'

'Mmm… they say AA can work.' He sounded less than convincing.

'Lewis, can I stay for a while? My flat has been turned upside down and I don't feel like fixing it yet.'

'Yeah, okay.'

*

That was the start of their relationship.

Lewis spent his days thinking about her and waited anxiously every night for her knock at his door. The way she said his name in her soft New Zealand accent was never so thrillingly

76

articulated. He was captivated by her and soon realised that he had considered himself a loner until she had come into his life.

Verity was equally enamoured with Lewis and very quickly their lives were inseparable. They spent time eating, watching TV and playing games. She was better than he; "God of War" was her choice, and he preferred "Red Dead Redemption 2". They laughed a lot and she invited him to view her artwork. She educated him about gothic art. She considered herself emo, a more modern take on gothic. She played music: "My Chemical Romance" was her favourite.

Change was happening to them both. As she completed her 12 steps, he became sober. She gave him the reason to fix up his life. He started looking for a job and life seemed good. Even her possession charge had been dropped.

One day, Verity came in looking less than happy. The inquest on Simon showed he had suffered a sudden heart attack. Toxicology findings were that ketamine, Mogadon and cocaine were present, and their combination was a contributing factor to his death.

Verity began sobbing, saying that it was her fault. She had felt sorry for him and offered him a bed for two or three nights, but after three weeks of him being high on coke, mazzies and alcohol he had disrupted her life and neighbours had been making complaints. The day he died she and Simon had a row and she told him to leave, to get out. When he had broken her door, she had raged at him. 'If only I had given him more time, or not left the flat…' she trailed off.

Lewis felt anxious; if this was confession time, he didn't want to join in. Instead, he held her tight. 'Verity, it wasn't your fault. You were kind to him, and he abused that. Simon knew what the dangers were. Anyone who uses knows that. He was a danger to you and to himself. He was a disaster waiting to happen. No one but you blames you.'

She looked so sad and vulnerable that it made his jaw tighten. But when she next spoke, he felt his anxiety soar. 'I always planned to go home to New Zealand when I finished my degree. My parents have a business and have offered to fund me to set up my own studio. Living here – knowing what happened to Si – is so hard. I need to go.'

Lewis was silent. The thought of losing her was too much. He had suffered loss before and knew how it had affected him.

'Lewis – you could come too, if you want to. I've told my parents about us. They would sponsor you. Think about it, please.'

He nodded, but his head was spinning.

Alone later, he felt afraid. Afraid to go back to that fateful day of the Gold Cup.

*

But he was curious about her. He walked towards her door and saw that the lock was broken. Quietly, he entered and saw a young man sprawled on the sofa. He instantly recognised him as one of the guys who had jumped on his back and stolen his wallet. He had him to thank for his aching purple jaw. Cautiously, he bent down and shook the man, but there was little response. He saw the needle already drawn up, the K's, plus his own wallet spread out on the side table. He picked up the wallet and withdrew a photograph. It was of Lewis and his younger brother, taken at school. Rage and grief engulfed him. It was a guy like this one, high on drugs, that had caused the car accident that had killed his brother.

The pain of his brother's death had devastated his parents and, unable to withstand their emotions as well as his own, he had left home. Only his friend Johnnie had dampened his pain. He slipped the photograph into his pocket and picked up the needle. Under his breath he said, 'This might keep you off people's back for a while longer.'

It had only taken a few moments of madness.

*

Lewis was in turmoil. His exciting relationship with Verity had blotted out his actions for a while but his nightmares had begun to haunt his days. He daren't tell her what he had done. He had already told her a lie about the purple bruising to his face. She would never trust him again. He daren't confess to the police. He hadn't meant Si to die but he could be charged with manslaughter. When Verity had called him to her flat, he had been as shocked as she was to find Si dead. He had to think straight.

What had he done with the photograph? It was the only thing that could place him in Verity's flat that day. What if it came to light that it was of him and his brother? Had Verity looked in his wallet and never mentioned seeing the photograph? He couldn't ask her without an explanation. Was Si already dead, and not just anaesthetised with K? Had he pre-empted him? After all, Si had taken K, was out of it, the coke ready to give him a high. Users used highs and lows all the time.

Had Si died coincidently when he had injected him? He couldn't be sure of anything, except that he loved Verity. He played out all the possible scenarios in his head.

That night he slept fitfully. He dreamt that Verity lay by his side, her arm wrapped around him.

Slowly the word "Truth" slithered down her arm and crept up to his throat, gripping like a tourniquet. He thrashed about, trying to free himself, and saw Verity crying over him, her hair all around him. The thumping of his heart awoke him. He was consumed with guilt and regret.

The next day Verity received a note:

Dear Verity,
I have to go away for a while.
It has been great knowing you.
Have a nice life in NZ.
Lewis.

WRONG PLACE, WRONG TIME

By JULIA GALE

It was the early summer of 1981 and my final day at school had arrived at last. I sat behind my school desk in the classroom and eagerly waited for the school bell to signal the end of the day. I ran out of the school gates for the last time and did not look back. At sixteen, I was overjoyed at the thought of not having to return to the place ever again, but also nervous about facing the future without having taken any exams. Other students had decided to stay behind on this last day, taking photos of themselves outside the building; a little keepsake to show off to future generations, maybe – but not for me. I merely ran until breathless and out of sight of the school. Finding a bench, I sat down, dumping my bag by my feet. I looked at it for a long moment, then I picked it up and, with all my strength, tossed it over a hedge and into a garden. It was a 'good riddance' moment, a 'free at last' moment and I shouted it aloud to the world. Then I continued my journey home, knowing that there would be no one there to greet me anyway. Mum and Dad would still be at work as it was only 3.30pm so I took the long route and thought about my time at school. *Had it really been all that bad?* I asked myself.

A memory came to mind; that of a school residential study break. We were on a beach collecting fossils. My friend Paul and I became bored and decided that we would try and spice things up a bit by giving one of the girls a scare. We found the biggest stone that we could find and slipped it down her back, telling her that it was a crab. She ran down the beach screaming so loudly that the teacher had to run after her and reassure her that it wasn't a crab at all. I chuckled, then stopped…there had been too many times like this. We were punished, of course. How many times had I been in front of the headteacher? I lost count…but then I didn't care that much either.

'Fun times indeed,' I said out loud to no one in particular, but I did not really believe that they were.

'*Backward, slow, badly behaved, the class clown, unteachable*' were some of the words my teachers used to describe me, and they were particularly fond of doing so at parents evening.

Their cruel words hit me hard, but not as hard as Dad did once we had returned home. My parents had high expectations for my sister and me; they both made plain their disappointment in me, but most particularly Dad.

The only GP within miles, Dad's practice was in a tiny, prefabricated hut in the centre of our village. Only two other people worked with him, Mrs Brown, his battle-axe of a receptionist, and Mrs Robbins, a kind but elderly nurse. He was an extremely busy man who worked long hard hours and he hoped that one day his only son would follow in his footsteps. He felt let down by my apparent lack of progress and interest at school. I prefer to think that he really did not understand me.

'What's wrong with the boy, why can't he be more like his sister?' he'd often asked my mother.

Her reply was always the same: 'He'll find his own way. He's just a little slower than the rest, that's all. We just need to be patient with him.' But Dad was not a patient man.

I really couldn't help it if I got my letters back to front and my numbers jumbled up and was still unable to read or write properly. It wasn't my fault and it wasn't his either; he had tried hard, but it was all too difficult. When I was younger, I had looked up to my dad. But these days, I lived in fear of him.

So, what was the point of anything? I asked myself that question. After all, the world was on the verge of a nuclear disaster if all the public information films on the television and the scary-looking leaflets that landed on my hallway doormat were to be believed.

Many of my classmates had decided to go to sixth form or try the new training scheme for young people that the school careers teacher had so eagerly promoted. £25 a week was a small fortune for many, but I had preferred to play kick-about in the street with Paul and Mike, the only two friends I had ever made. They were like me, or so I thought. So, when both of them told me of their plans to sign up for the work scheme, I felt betrayed and very angry. I suppose it was because it meant, to me, that we were no longer children playing in the street and were now about to face the world as adults.

Unreasonably, I thought: *'How could they do this to me?'* From now on I was going to be the master of my own destiny and nobody was going to stand in my way.

'Fred, Fred. Please stop, just for a minute!' a familiar voice called out to me.

I was in two minds whether to ignore the voice calling me from behind but decided to turn around anyway. It was Paul.

'Yes? What do you want?' I asked Paul abruptly. 'I really don't want anything more to do with you. Go away!'

'I'm sorry Fred, really I am! So, thought I'd try and make it up to you. I found these in the teacher's bin today. There were loads of them left over, so I thought one or two or all of them wouldn't be missed.' He handed me a small piece of paper. It was a ticket for the school leavers' disco. I glanced briefly at the ticket and then at Paul.

'Why have you given me this?' I demanded. 'You know how I hate discos.' But I knew that, with a little gentle coaxing, Paul could persuade me to come, albeit reluctantly.

'I am going to it. Mike is as well. Like you, we don't really like discos, you know we don't, but I promise you this one will be a laugh. All the teachers will be there…a chance to make fun of them perhaps? Get our own back. I'll bring some cans of Top Deck. That will give us give us some courage beforehand.'

I grinned at that. Top Deck was our favourite beer-flavoured soft drink. It was just like Paul to think of little things like having a few drinks beforehand and, to be honest, I had started to miss his and Mike's company, even though it had only been a couple of weeks since we split up.

'Ok then, maybe I'll think about it,' I replied, folding the ticket and putting it in my trouser pocket. I hoped that Mum would put my trousers in the twin tub without checking my pockets first.

'I'll take that as a yes then. Shall I?' Paul replied cheekily, muttering a quick 'See you then!' as he cycled away.

*

But Mum didn't forget to check my trouser pockets as I had hoped. In fact, the ticket fell out of my trouser pocket and onto the floor. I picked it up and decided to show it to Mum. She knew that I didn't like parties. In fact, any kind of social event at all. Ever since I was a toddler, she often had to take me into another room where it was quieter. She had never understood why I was so different from my sister.

I didn't have to go, of course, if I didn't want to. But Mum did try to make it sound like something special and promised to buy me some new clothes. She knew that by promising me new togs I may be persuaded to go. After all, it would be a good way to celebrate the end of an era and the start of adulthood. Whatever that held for me. I guessed that she wasn't too sure, but she hoped it would signal the start of a better future. So I gave in and rang the boys to say that I would go after all.

The day of the leavers' disco came around far too soon for me, but I put on the new clothes that Mum had bought me, baggy trousers and a pirate shirt, and waited for my friends to come and pick me up. I rang Paul and Mike to confirm that I was still going, although I had my doubts. The thought of having a few cigarettes and a couple of Top Decks beforehand gave me some comfort. We walked the long route to school. We preferred to walk; my mum did offer to drive us there but we declined and when we finally arrived, the party was already in full swing. It was just as I had expected: the music was deafening and the lights glaring, almost blinding. They were reminders of why I disliked going to parties in the first place.

The girls sat in one corner of the hall, looking bored. They were wearing silly "rara" skirts and legwarmers; the boys sat at the opposite end of the hall looking just as bored as the girls. They wore much the same as my friends and me, so we didn't look too out of place, much to my relief.

About halfway through, the music was stopped, and the normal lights turned back on. Break time, when the sandwiches, cheese and pineapple on sticks, sausage rolls, Twiglets and nuts were put on the tables by the tired-looking catering staff. Before we were allowed to help ourselves, one of the catering staff told us to dispose of the cocktail sticks sensibly afterwards and warned us not to stab each other with them. She had seen the damage a cocktail stick could do and she wasn't going to let that happen again. Honestly, how old did she think we were, five?

For us, it was an opportunity to go outside, pop down to the local shop and buy some more Top Decks, have some more smokes and generally chill out. The loud music left my ears buzzing and my head thumping. I longed for some fresh air. But first I had to find Paul and Mike. They had wandered off somewhere, leaving me in the crowd watching Mr. Cook and Miss Leclerc making complete idiots of themselves dancing to *Night Fever*. Mr. Cook really fancied himself as the next John Travolta, though he was fat and over forty and had a leg injury. He wasn't doing too bad a job at it until he stumbled and tripped over a handbag that had been left lying on the dance floor. Once he had picked himself up and dusted himself down, he held the handbag above his head and demanded to know which clumsy idiot had forgotten to pick it up. He expected one of the girls to respond, of course, but when nobody came forward, he stomped back to his seat in the corner and threw the bag back onto the dance floor. A few minutes later, Miss Leclerc returned. Looking shame-faced and more than slightly embarrassed, she picked up the bag; it was hers all along. When she heard about Mr Cook's unfortunate accident, she immediately went to apologise to him. We all thought it was great to see one of the teachers make a mistake.

It was after that little bit of excitement that I found Paul and Mike standing by the back door close to the toilets. They were talking to a girl dressed top to toe in black. I had not seen her before. She was tall, taller than the boys, and they seemed small and inconsequential beside her. She had dyed jet black hair and black eyeliner; a gothic look that stood out amongst the bright rara skirts of the other girls. She obviously liked being different; I could tell that it didn't bother her. I wished that I had the same confidence. Even though there was nothing remotely cute about her, I found myself liking her, especially when she turned and looked at me with those dark eyes; there was something quite mysterious about them. I was fascinated and wanted to find out more but I found my legs had turned to jelly and refused to move. By the time I regained the feeling in my legs, she had finished her conversation with Mike and Paul and disappeared out of the exit door. I was disappointed and wondered how she could have known the two boys; until now, they had spent most of their days either at school or hanging around with me.

'Where did you go? Did you see what happened to Mr. Cook a few minutes ago?' I asked. I really wanted to ask about the girl but skirted around it until I felt the time was right. They both said that they had heard the laughter and commotion inside the hall, but had not seen it. They didn't seem too bothered about missing it, which was unusual for them. Perhaps the girl in black had bewitched them as much as she had me. I could not wait any longer.

'Who was that girl you were talking to? I've not seen her round here before. You seem to be pretty friendly with her...have one of you got a girlfriend and not told me about it?' I asked, only half-jokingly.

'Oh no, she's just a friend of someone I know,' Mike replied. But I felt that there was something they were trying to hide from me. After all, I had known them for a long time. Surely they knew that I'd find out some way or the other.

Paul suggested we go outside, which I was by now longing for. The break had finished, and the party had started up again. The noise was even louder and was making my headache worse. We went to the shop, bought some more cans of Top Deck and made our way slowly back to the school. We figured that nobody would notice that we weren't actually in the hall, so we could take our time and then slip back in towards the end, pretending that we had been there all the time.

I stayed outside to finish a cigarette. I was stubbing it out and about to go back in when I felt someone tap me on the shoulder. I jumped back and came face to face with the girl in black. This time I could see her face more clearly; although it was smothered in heavy make-up, I could see that she was as darkly lovely as my first impression had given me.

'Hello, Fred,' she said, quietly. Then, casually, she offered me another cigarette from a newly opened packet.

'How do you know my name?' I asked her, taking the cigarette. I didn't really want it, to be honest, but suddenly felt obliged. We took our cigarettes to the bike shed.

85

'I've seen you around the school with Mike and the other boy,' she said. 'What's his name?'

'His name is Paul,' I ventured. 'What do you want with us? I saw you chatting to them at breaktime. I have not seen you around the school. Are you even meant to be here?' I asked her suspiciously.

'I'm a friend of Mike's cousin and I'm new here,' she told me. 'Mike promised his cousin that he'd show me around the town and introduce me to his friends. But he hasn't really kept his part of the bargain. It's not easy being in a new place and not knowing anyone. So, I thought I'd introduce myself. My name is Guiella. If you think that's strange, check out my surname – it's Fawkes.'

We talked. Perhaps the Top Decks, even with the little alcohol they contained, were loosening both our tongues. She told me she had been adopted by her aunt and uncle. They had thought about changing her name to plain Ella as they thought the "Gui" bit was a bit odd, especially with their surname being Fawkes. But her birth mother had demanded that her sister keep her daughter's name as it was. Gui could not recall her mother, and her aunt and uncle never saw or heard from her again either. She was now living with just her aunt as her uncle died a couple of years ago and that was their reason for moving to a new area. I was amused; who in their right mind would name their daughter after Guy Fawkes? Someone with a strange sense of humour, I supposed. I hoped that she wasn't tempted to be like her namesake.

I thought at first that it was a little odd that Mike had never mentioned he had a cousin. But then he rarely spoke about his family at all, so it sort of made sense. Why would this girl want to be friends with us? I had already figured that she would not be the sort of person my parents would like me to hang around with anyway. But even though I was curious about this strange girl and, for some reason, felt a little sorry for her, something told me to stay well away…but I knew that I would not.

Guiella suddenly pulled a small bottle from her bag and offered me a swig of whisky. I refused and wondered where she had got it from but I was getting to the stage where things she said and did were not so surprising. She shrugged and moved away into the darkness, and my eyes followed her until I could no longer make out her form.

At that point, Mr. Cook came alongside me. I suspect it was for a sneaky ciggie of his own, but it seemed that he had been watching the two of us closely. I was sort of touched when he quietly advised me against getting involved with her, as she had "trouble" written on her forehead. He obviously knew more about her than I did. I reassured him, untruthfully, that I had no intention of seeing her anymore. He seemed happy with my response, and he turned away; I guess he felt, perhaps, that he had fulfilled the duties of a teacher and done his bit.

I spent the rest of the party looking for Paul and Mike, but they were nowhere to be seen. So, I just sat in the corner supping a bottle of Coca-Cola, watching as Miss Leclerc and Mr. Cook made fools of themselves again, this time smooching to a soppy record by a new band named after some German World War 2 prison camp.

The party finished at last and I was one of the first out of the door. I saw that Guiella was waiting in the shadows for me and, suddenly nervous, I tried to avoid her, urgently looking for Mum's car in amongst all the others.

'Fred,' she called from the darkness. 'Fred, can I have your number? I like you and want to hang out with you over the summer.' She followed me into the car park; there was no means of escaping her…I was relieved to see that Mum had just turned up and was now waving at me, beckoning me towards her. I didn't want her to see me with a girl, least of all, a creepy goth girl, attractive as she was. I ran quickly towards Mum and the car. I didn't give Guiella my number and part of me, but not all, hoped that she wouldn't try to follow me or contact me again.

'Did you have a good time, Fred?' Mum asked as we drove down the road. I was still a little breathless from all that running but replied anyway. I didn't want to lie and tell her that everything went really well, but also didn't want her to know about Guiella. So, I told her about Mr. Cook and Miss Leclerc and the catering staff telling us what to do with cocktail sticks. We both had a good laugh.

*

87

A number of weeks had passed since the incident with Guiella and by then I had almost, but not quite, forgotten about the girl in black. Mike and Paul had started their training and Mum and Dad were at work all week, leaving my sister and me to look after the house.

I was at home alone the day I received the phone call. I could have let our new posh answering machine get it, but I was feeling more than a little bored and frustrated and in need of something to do, so I answered it myself. I did not recognise her voice at first and it took me a few seconds to realise exactly who was at the other end of the line.

'Guiella? How did you get my number?' For some reason, my voice shook a little and I tried to control it by sounding surprised at her call.

'It wasn't too difficult. I looked up Dr. Grimes in the phone book and put two and two together. It lists both the surgery number and your home number, you know; there aren't that many people with the surname Grimes around here.'

'Fair enough…but what do you want?' I said.

'Are you free on Friday?' she asked. 'Cos, as you know, the others are working now and I'm bored with nobody to hang around with. I thought you might be feeling the same way?' Not waiting for an answer, she then told me to meet her outside The Bridge public house in the village at 12pm on Friday.

I hesitated, then found myself saying: 'Well, I…ok…I'll see you then.' I put the phone down.

I worried about our meeting all week. There was no reason but I felt somehow that I should have been stronger and turned this invitation down. I decided not to mention the phone call to anyone. Mr. Cook's warning rang in my head. Where were Paul and Mike when I needed them?

*

Friday found me outside The Bridge at 12pm. Guiella had not yet arrived. I waited for a half-hour longer than I should have, and yet something stopped me from leaving. I paced up and down and wondered what she could possibly want with me. I was beginning to think that I was on a fool's mission and began to walk away, relieved and yet somehow disappointed, when she suddenly arrived; I did not notice from where. She had a faint smile on her heavily made-up face and offered no apology for being late. She was silent for a few moments.

'Are you hungry?' she asked, eventually. She looked at me from the side, almost slyly, then turned her full gaze upon me; later, I came to recognise that she did so each time she wanted me to go along with something she proposed. I wasn't particularly hungry but told her that I was, as if this might please her, but that I didn't have any money on me. At that, she just smiled and told me that she knew how to get food, or anything she wanted, when it was needed – and she would show me how. I suddenly found that I was hungry after all.

Guiella chose a shop, a small local store that seemed to take her fancy, and when we entered, she told me to grab a basket. I followed her around the aisles like an obedient puppy. She went from shelf to shelf swapping the price labels while I did exactly as she asked – I kept a lookout, making sure that nobody would notice her. It seemed unnecessary, as there was only one other customer in the shop and a bored-looking woman sitting behind the till. Soon we had a basket full of goodies and we took it to the counter. The woman keyed in each item, occasionally looking at the list of prices beside the till. She looked puzzled. Of course, she knew something was not quite right, but waited until the last item in our basket before looking at us. I could not hold her gaze but Guiella was not one to be cowed by a shop girl, or anyone else, I suspected.

'Hold on a moment, please, I need to check something with the manager,' she said. Then she reached down to press the button underneath the till; we both knew what that meant.

Guiella nudged me. 'Run!' she whispered. I bolted for it but even as we ran for the door Guiella grabbed some items, laughing as she did so. I didn't feel like laughing myself.

We stopped only when we knew we weren't being pursued and ate what food had been taken in a local park.

'That was fun and easy,' announced Guiella once we had got rid of the evidence. *Easy?* I hadn't found it easy at all, but – I had to be honest with myself – the adrenalin had kicked in. It made my heart beat faster. It was exciting – and I wanted more. Despite myself, I had enjoyed the experience. More important than all this was that Guiella seemed happy with me; she suggested that we meet up again a few days later – and I agreed. I liked the idea of seeing her again, she was attractive and fun…no, not fun, there was too much of an edge to her for that.

We walked slowly back home, but not before Guiella had scrambled onto the precipice of the bridge that linked the main road into the village. A stupid and dangerous thing to do, but it didn't seem to bother her in the least. She walked, calm and unhurried, from one end to the other with a drop on one side steep enough to break her neck. She then invited me to do the same, and when I refused she called me a coward. Her laugh rang in my ears long after she had departed. But that still didn't put me off her.

*

I counted the days until our next meeting; she was all that I could think of. I couldn't ring her as she had told me that her aunt had not yet had a phone installed and she would call me again from a phone box. My heart skipped a beat every time the phone rang and I hoped that she would not call on a day my parents were at home. When the call finally came, my parents were at work and yet I still found myself lowering my voice as if in conspiracy; perhaps it was, in a way. She told me to meet her and there was never any chance that I wouldn't.

I made my way to meet her that same morning. We had arranged to meet outside Woolworths and this time she was waiting for me. She nodded and I followed her into the store, where she headed for the record section. In silence, we flicked through the vinyl albums, which I could see were far too costly for me. The cheapest was two pounds – four whole weeks' allowance – and that was if I bothered to help Mum around the house. Guiella noticed that I'd been looking at a record by my favourite band for quite a while.

Finally, she spoke. 'Do you want that one?' she asked. I shrugged my shoulders and told her that it was far too expensive. She took out her purse, opened it and pulled out a wad of crisp green pound notes. I did not even bother to ask her where she got the money from. I was more concerned about how I would

90

explain the record to my parents, and I still hadn't told them about Guiella.

The summer was long and hot and our meetings throughout it became increasingly frequent. Before long I had mastered the art of price swapping.

*

It wasn't just price swapping, though. There was out-and-out shoplifting, anything that got us a few quid, but there were other things just done for the hell of it: drinking, setting fire to litter bins, low-level stuff. No violence, mind you, but generally creating trouble wherever we went.

It may seem amazing but we were only caught once, by the local beat bobby, PC White.

Guiella and I were just leaving the Co-Op with a few things under our clothes when he walked in. He was sharp-eyed and quick and must have known what we were up to as he grabbed us both and demanded that we hand everything back to the shop manager. We had no choice other than to do as we were told. He took us outside and warned us not to do it again, as he would not hesitate to arrest us next time. This was fairer than we deserved and we walked away, me shame-faced and relieved, but Guiella laughed once we had turned the corner. It was the sheer brass of her that both frightened me and kept me coming back for more.

You would think by now that I would have cottoned on to the fact that Guiella was not good for me. In fact, I had but it didn't matter; I really didn't notice how like her I'd become. I began dying my hair black and chose to wear only dark clothing, sometimes stuff that Guiella and I had stolen. My attitude changed but I noticed that hers did too. Guiella was now demanding that I spend every day with her and most nights. It was becoming increasingly difficult for me to explain my absences to Mum and Dad; what else could I do but lie to them? They knew that something was not right.

*

Late one night I crept out of the house to see Guiella; it was not unusual for us to meet after midnight now. The few lamp lights were glowing orange like the lit ends of the cigarettes she

91

smoked, and the streets were cold and quiet; I saw shadows in alleys and doorways but not a soul otherwise.

She had rung me earlier in the day asking if I knew where my dad kept his key for the surgery. This disturbed me...but I was now beyond questioning her about anything she had planned for us. So, I borrowed the key...no, let me be honest for the first time in quite a while...I stole the key from my dad's jacket pocket and made my way in those still streets to the surgery.

Guiella was never the best at greetings; it was usually just a nod, but today there was even less. She appeared agitated when I arrived and just held out her hand for the key. When I hesitated, she snatched it from me and started to fumble with the lock. In the dark, opening the door was not easy and neither of us had a torch. Finally, we slipped inside and I turned on the lights briefly to disarm the alarm. Dad once told Mum, my sister and me the number in confidence, just in case we ever had to use it. Guiella hissed at me to turn the light out again. I felt that something was very wrong.

I watched in horror as Guiella suddenly went on the rampage throughout the surgery, cursing me for not helping her; I had no idea what she meant. The only light was coming from the street lights outside, making it difficult to see anything. How Guiella managed to find her way around, I'll never know. Somehow, we reached the nurse's room, which was locked.

'Open the door!' she yelled at me. I was somewhat taken aback at being shouted at. She had never spoken to me like that before.

'I don't have the key.' My reply angered her even more.

'I need to know where your dad hides the Blueys,' she said, trying to keep herself calm. I looked down at her hands and noticed that she was wearing gloves. Her hands were shaking slightly. Not understanding what she meant by Blueys, I asked her to explain.

She stared nastily at me as she replied with more than a hint of scorn. 'DRUGS, you idiot! Any sort of drugs. You don't seriously think that I'd really waste my time with you if I'd not heard that your dad was a doctor? You didn't really think that I would hang around with a cretin like you? Where did you think I got my money from – selling lollipops?'

I stood in stunned silence as Guiella turned towards the door, kicking the debris she had caused across the floor. Before she left, she turned to me, and her final words hit me like a bombshell.

'Oh, there's more...do you want to know the real reason I moved here, and why I latched on to you that day?' Miserably, I nodded in response. 'Revenge,' she said, quietly. 'I wanted to get close to you because of your dad.'

I was close to tears. 'Why?' I asked.

'Your dad killed my mum, as good as. She moved here after having me adopted. A new life, without me...but I know she would have come back for me eventually, I just – well, I just know it. Shortly afterwards, she became sick and went to see your dad – several times. Each time he dismissed her worries and gave her a prescription for medication that did no good. By the time he referred her to a consultant at the hospital it was way too late.'

I thought about Dad, always so meticulous and proud of his profession. Always critical of me; of my mistakes, my lack of ambition. But I didn't take any pleasure from whatever mistake he had made, because that is what it would have been: a horrible one, but a mistake nonetheless. A lapse, an error of judgment. I know what those are like.

'Who told you all this? And why have you waited until now?'

'As soon as I turned eighteen, my aunt told me. She had kept contact with Mum, even attended her funeral...without me. I never knew my mother...it was all her fault for keeping her from me. I tried to find a job so I could afford to move here, close to the man that killed my mum. Nobody would employ me. So, I resorted to drug dealing. Business was good and within a year I could afford to rent a place.'

'How did your aunt feel when you told her that you were moving here?' I asked, starting to feel very uneasy.

'She didn't have time to tell me. I kept quiet but was angry, so angry that the first chance I got I torched the house and ran.' She put her hand on the door. 'Got any more questions for me? Cos I'm done with talking now.' She lit up a cigarette and waved it at me. 'You and your family, watch your backs. It's Bonfire

Night tomorrow. You know my name…and now you know what I'm capable of too, don't you?'

All I could do was stare in horror at her as she slammed the door behind her.

*

I stayed in the surgery for hours. Her words remained in my head and I ran over them again and again. What did she mean by "watch our backs"?

I was at a loss as to what I should do next. My first instinct was to tidy up, put the chairs back, close the drawers, put everything in its rightful place and make it look as though nothing had happened, but I left the surgery as it was, as if a break-in had occurred. Warily, I headed out into the night for home and when I got there, I found the house still silent and dark with nobody awake. I slipped the keys back, went to my bedroom and lay down. I didn't sleep much.

The next day was Saturday the fifth of November – Bonfire Night. Mum, Dad and my sister were busy preparing for the annual firework party that we hosted in our back garden. I was in no mood to help; instead, I spent the day in my room, thinking about the events of the night before.

When the evening finally rolled around, I was persuaded to go downstairs by the appetising smell of hotdogs and burgers. I'd not eaten all day.

I ate my fill but didn't mingle with the guests. Instead, something drew me out into the night and my footsteps turned towards the surgery in the village. The air was thick and acrid with smoke from people's bonfires; the sky itself was alive with flashes and starbursts of colour and the crackle of fireworks was like gunfire.

Ahead, through the smog, something was emerging. I waited. It was the outline of someone running towards me from the direction of Dad's surgery and I knew who it was even before I could see them clearly. It was Guiella. Fawkes.

I wanted to run and hide, but it was too late for that, she had seen me. Before I could say anything, she had pressed something into my hand. I saw that it was an empty petrol can. She looked at me just once, but it was enough for me to see that she was smiling, her eyes lit up with what could have been triumph, I

94

guess. Before I could speak or make myself move, she had gone; she disappeared as quickly as she arrived.

Instinct made me suddenly run. Not home, but onward, towards the surgery. I could see light and flames too large to be a bonfire. Sure enough, it was ablaze, the flames leaping upwards in red and yellow streaks. If this had been what she meant, she had carried out her threat. For a long while I stood frozen to the spot, helpless and in shock as the building burned. I did not move even when the sound of sirens grew louder and stopped behind me. A firm voice told me to drop the can. I did so and then a pair of handcuffs were clamped on me and I was led to a waiting police car while a dozen firefighters fought the blaze. I didn't protest, and I didn't have any hope for the surgery. It was at that point I felt that Guiella Fawkes had gained her revenge.

ROVER'S RETURN

By C.G. Harris

If the moon hadn't been at its fullest, I might not have seen where he dropped it. And, if he hadn't treated me so well that day, I might have been inclined to leave it 'zactly where it was. But…well, one good turn deserves another, and I was sure as eggs is eggs, he wouldn't want to lose that thing; he seemed to love waving it around so. I've seen him pointing it at Missus with the strangest dang look on his face and his eyes and lips all screwed up tight. I never liked the way she shook and covered her face with her hands when he did that, nor the smell on his breath when he pulled me to him; when he was that way, I made to slink away most times and hide under the porch.

Come to it, I ain't seen Missus around, not since that helluva bang yesterday evenin'; it dang near bust my ears.

Anyways, this mornin' he's up with the rooster crowing in the yard and loadin' up the truck with somethin' big and long all rolled up in a blanket and he don't come back 'till the sun's high; he was looking kinda satisfied when he did.

He washed his hands thorough then and fed me good, and I sat contented with him 'till dark. All the while he kept turning this thing over and over, all solid and heavy looking and flickering yellow and red from the firelight. Then some cars pulled up and the flickering turned blue and there were some real heavy footsteps coming up the path – plenty of them. He rushed up and hightailed it through the backyard and I followed hard on by 'till I seed he dropped that thing in some shrub and kept on movin' fast; so, I picked it up and took it back home. I figured he'd be hellish pleased with me to find it there waiting for him when he got back.

I was double-pleased when one of the big men in blue took it gently from me and stroked me. He put it in a see-through bag.

"Attaboy, Rover," he said. Though I don't know how he knew my name.

THE CHINA DOG

By Glynne Covell

Gillian stared through the window, looking but not seeing, more absorbed in the droplets of rain making rivers on the glass. Slowly, slowly meandering downwards, going nowhere, like tears. Translucent, meaningless and insignificant. Just like me, she thought. Empty. Hollow. At 58, Gillian felt old before her time, having been together for 40 years with Gerald, a bombastic and coercive man who she had begun to dislike within a few years of marriage. A dislike which had gradually turned to hatred.

Gillian checked the oven. The chicken was roasting to golden brown and the potatoes crisping nicely with the goose fat. Gerald's boss, Mark and wife, Serena, were coming to dinner. Always a boring evening for Gillian with endless talk of work. She would sit quietly cringing as Gerald blew his own trumpet. Serena was the firm's accountant: a voluptuous and confident young woman who took an active interest in the growing business, an innovative security systems company.

She heard footfall on the stairs and then tuneless whistling as Gerald entered the lounge, stopping at the fireplace, as usual, to adjust the china dog on the mantelpiece. Bloody dog, thought Gillian. It was a big bone of contention. She'd been given the large, hideous, brown and white china cocker spaniel as a present from Gerald's mother for her birthday. She despised the monstrosity almost as much as she had hated her mother-in-law, recently deceased, who had left an enormous fortune to her only son. She often tried to push the ornament to one side of the mantelpiece to give it a less important place, but Gerald would continually readjust it to centre stage.

The bell interrupted her thoughts and Gerald turned up the volume of his excruciating whistling as he went to answer the door. "Mark, Serena, lovely to see you. Come in!" he cried with great gusto. "Gilly, they're here," he called. "Hope you've got that champers on ice."

97

Gillian joined them, greeting them politely but a little less enthusiastically. She was aware that there had been a brief adulterous affair between Gerald and Serena some time ago but she believed that Mark was totally unaware of this. She offered her best welcoming smile, but cringed at Gerald calling her Gilly in front of them. He always did this as a show of affection in front of people; he also enjoyed the fact that Gillian loathed it.

After a glass of champagne to toast the successful launch of the new contract with an up-and-coming car showroom, the conversation, mainly about the business, flowed, during which Gillian sat with a fixed smile, an occasional nod, merely listening.

At one point, she did attempt to steer the evening away from work. "I'm thinking of joining an art group," she interjected enthusiastically. "There's a new class starting in the village and I really feel I should get my watercolours out again." Gillian had managed a first in a History of Art degree many years before but had allowed Gerald to convince her that home-keeping was far more important than seeking work and fulfilling her personal ambitions.

Her comment was at first met by silence.

"Hey, Gilly," exclaimed Serena, slavishly following Gerald's lead in calling her the dreaded shortened form of her name. "Good for you, girl. You'll probably find the inspiration you need from likeminded art lovers."

Gerald, who was more taken with Serena's low-cut dress than his wife's comment, changed the subject. "Well, as I was saying, Mark, next year we may well have to look into larger premises if these new contracts keep coming in," he said, raising his voice as if to quell any future interruptions from Gillian.

Gillian felt her face redden but managed to control the rising volcanic anger. She reminded herself that he had had a number of affairs in the past and had only slowed down now because of his heart condition. She sat there for a further five minutes listening to Gerald rant on about his business prowess and then excused herself, with a beaming smile, to tend to the dinner in the kitchen.

"May I help, Gilly?" asked Serena, putting down her glass.

"No, Serena, I'm fine, thank you. Have another glass of champagne while I finish off."

"Well said, Gilly," exclaimed Gerald enthusiastically as he jumped up to refill the glasses. "Perfect hostess, our Gilly," he added condescendingly.

Gerald came out as soon as she called to help her transport the many dishes of food to the table. "Got to help the little lady," he joked. "Keep the chef happy at all times."

"Looks gorgeous, Gilly, first class," said Serena.

"Yes, she certainly has improved over the years. I think my dear mum helped her to where she is now with her culinary expertise. Wouldn't you agree, Gilly?"

"Well, I have actually always had…" she began.

"Now, Mark, what do you feel about offsetting transport costs against the new budget?" asked Gerald, abruptly cutting short her reply.

Gillian sat down, her heart pounding. Keep calm, she told herself. Breathe deeply.

"Delicious dinner, Gilly, but the gravy is rather thin today. Would you like to go and thicken it? Don't want to spoil the ship for a ha'porth of tar, do we?" laughed Gerald, who always found cliched jokes extremely amusing.

"No problem," she said, dutifully, as she put down her knife and fork and took the gravy jug back into the kitchen.

Once away from the table, she screwed up her face in anger. In the kitchen, she eyed the carving knife by the chicken. Aggressively, she grabbed it and, using the knife as a dagger, struck down into the chicken carcass with such force that the noise of knife on metal carving tray resulted in an ear-piercing high-pitched scraping. Again, and again, she plunged the knife into the remaining chicken flesh, stabbing viciously with pent up rage, reducing the flesh to shreds. It was no longer a chicken; it was Gerald's head…or maybe Serena's. Putting down the knife, Gillian closed her eyes and, taking deep breaths, gradually calmed down and controlled her shaking hands. It had been a satisfying episode, she thought, as she returned with the gravy boat.

"Well done, Gilly, much better," said Gerald, patronisingly. "If at first you don't succeed, try, try again." He laughed and patted her hand.

Serena turned towards her and smiled. "I'm not complaining, Gilly. I hardly have any gravy myself. Beautiful meal though. Absolutely delicious."

Oh God, thought Gillian, it sounds as if she really means it.

Time dragged on with discussion of the ethics of removing staff who were deemed not worthy to be on the payroll together with new ideas about expanding trade.

"We must be on our way, I'm afraid. Busy day tomorrow with our lad, Marcus having an early start for a school trip and then we have theatre in the evening," said Mark, "but a most enjoyable evening, guys. Wonderful meal, Gilly, and apologies if we've talked shop."

Gillian smiled, relieved to see an end to the evening. Tomorrow was Monday and Gerald would be back to work.

The dishwasher loaded and table cleared, Gerald announced he was ready for bed as he had a big day ahead. Lots of redundancies to announce.

"Okay, I'll finish off down here and read for a while. My book is due back at the library tomorrow," answered Gillian.

Five minutes later, a deafening, reverberating crash echoed through the house. She calmly put down her book, took off her glasses and looked up. An agonising cry from upstairs followed. It was Gerald.

"Gerald, what's happened?" she called up the stairs.

No reply.

Entering their bedroom, her first sight was the overturned bookcase; books and ornaments thrown off and the lamp shattered on the floor. But she could not see Gerald.

"Gerald…Gerald?"

A weak whispering voice called out her name and then she saw Gerald's arm as he attempted to raise it from the floor where he was lying on the other side of the bed.

"Tablets," he whimpered. "Where…where are my tablets?"

Gillian's heart beat faster as she walked over to him. He looked up pleadingly, his face ghostly white, his lips tinged blue. Clutching his chest in obvious excruciating pain, he held out a hand to Gillian as he begged for help. There was a large gash on his forehead where he had obviously knocked his head in the fall.

"Here they are, Gerald," she answered, calmly holding up the bottle of tablets above her head.

"Give…give me…." Gerald slurred, holding out his hand in desperation.

"Come and get them, Gerald," commanded Gillian as she placed them back in her pocket. "That's a very nasty-looking cut on your head, you know. I'll go downstairs and call for an ambulance."

Downstairs, she took the phone from the holder in the hall and went into the lounge to make the call. But first she needed another glass of champagne. It was opened and a shame to let it go to waste. As she walked into the room, the china dog caught her eye. She stopped to look at it, her eyes narrowing critically. Moving forward, she pushed the offending ornament further back whereby it became slightly hidden by a candlestick. But…maybe it could even stand at the other end, she thought. Possibly it would have even less impact there. No, damn it, she said to herself. It's bloody ugly! With that thought, she deliberately pushed it off the shelf and it crashed into smithereens before her. She smiled as she looked down at brown and white china pieces scattered in the hearth. She breathed in slowly and deeply. A wonderful feeling of relief and contentment washed over her.

Returning to the bedroom, she found Gerald face down. Not wanting to touch him, she simply nudged him with her slipper. No movement. Another nudge, more akin to a kick. No sign of breathing.

Gillian laughed. A thought flashed through her mind that one should never kick a man when he's down.

Taking her time, she slowly descended the stairs, after making sure she replaced Gerald's heart tablets where they should have been. She rehearsed the conversation she would be having with emergency services and the paramedics. Gillian would be convincing as a grieving widow.

The paramedics wrote 'dead on arrival' on their notes. A suspected heart attack. The doctor had since been and given a certification of death and Gerald had been taken away by the undertakers.

As the paramedics left the house, they asked Gillian again if she was sure she was alright and if there was a relative or a friend who she could call to come over to be with her. No, she would be alright, she said. No, there was no one. She was quite adamant. She would be okay.

"Strong lady there," said George, the paramedic as he closed the door. "Very stoic. She'll be fine."

Gillian smiled as she congratulated herself, recalling that a drama teacher had commented on her acting qualities at school. She was more than pleased with her performance when the ambulance had arrived.

Maybe I'll look out for an amateur dramatics group as well as getting back to my art, she thought.

POLLY RODGERS AND THE DODGY COTTAGE

By Jan Brown

"We're really sorry, Polly," Stella from personnel had told me at lunchtime on Friday. I'd stared at her heavily lacquered hair and wondered how she managed to smoke without regularly setting herself alight. "We'll obviously provide you with a good reference." She'd smiled at me vaguely, patted said hair and trotted off, no doubt in search of her next cigarette.

So that had been on the Friday and instead of hitting the employment agencies, here I was on Monday morning, mooching around, telling some random old lady how much I loved her house.

"That's a lovely thing to say, my dear, thank you. I call it Pleasant View Cottage." She stopped sweeping the pavement outside her property and leant on the broom. "My nephew pops round quite regularly to help me out with things, you know. Do you know him?" she asked, leaning in towards me.

I caught a scent of Old English Lavender talc, which my mum had loved. "Erm no, I don't think so. Does he live locally?"

"Yes. He's a very keen gardener, loves his exotic plants."

I raised my voice. "Does he live near to you in case of emergencies?"

"Oh yes, he's always popping round, can't keep him away, bless him. Good day, dear." She nodded at me, turned slowly and disappeared inside, closing the front door behind her.

As I stood alone on the village green, I looked towards the spire of the distant church. It was a lovely little village, less than 10 miles from central London and, unbelievably, very near to where Rob and I lived. It had cemented its village status through the construction of a 1950s bypass, which had effectively cut it off from passing traffic and made it rather pointless for drivers to take the single road through it.

The 2019 version of the high street had a collection of essential shops rather than quaint ones: a newsagent, fish and chip shop, chemist and Indian restaurant. The latest addition was a tearoom, definitely the nearest thing to quaint, and, further down the road, one could also get one's canine family member groomed, but the tailor of many years' standing had now closed down, a solitary dummy standing forlornly in the shop window.

At one end of the high street was a set of traffic lights with various travelling options; turn left and in 15 minutes on a good day you would reach Bromley. At the other end of the high street, if you followed the footpath past the Victorian church you would quickly find yourself in open countryside.

I crouched down to stroke a fat black and white cat I had noticed earlier sauntering towards me. "Hello gorgeous," I whispered, smoothing my hand through his thick plush fur. Then I sighed. No more reason to delay. I had to face the music and tell Rob the bad news.

A brisk 20-minute walk home took me back to Orpington's over-developed environs and away from the peace and isolation of the village.

"Rob, I'm home."

"Polly, hi, I didn't realise you were back. In fact, how long have you been back? Where are you back from?"

His blue eyes had that now familiar slightly glazed look and my nose wrinkled at the pungent aroma pervading the summer house, but this had been the agreement reached after much debate: keep it out of the house and I might be able to ignore it.

"I just walked back from the village. What about you? Have you had a good day?"

"Yes, not bad actually, I've had a piece accepted by the New Statesman so just celebrating."

"Ah, well done Rob, that's great. Are you coming in for dinner?"

"I'll be in soon."

"Actually, I've got something to tell you and it might be best to do it now as you're in a good mood." I twisted my plait of thick brown hair anxiously around my fingers.

"What's up, Pol? You're not pregnant, are you?"

"Ha ha! No, that really would be disastrous. I've been made redundant from the solicitors; I've got no job." I felt really tearful. Saying the words aloud brought it home to me.

"I'm sorry, honey. I know you enjoyed working there. Don't worry too much, I can look after us until you find something else." He drew me into a bear hug. "Is there much out there?"

"I don't know," I admitted. "I spent the day wandering around the village. Got chatting to a lovely old lady outside the white house, which she informs me is called Pleasant View Cottage. You know I've always fancied that place, but fat chance of that now."

"Come on, Polly, you've just said you don't know. There might actually be something in the village to tide you over. You should ask around and, in the meantime," Rob grabbed my hand, "let's go and eat."

*

On Tuesday, I walked into the village again to sit in the tearoom; probably not the best idea when you've just lost your job. I sipped at my Earl Grey and looked absentmindedly through the latest News Shopper, which, these days, mainly consisted of adverts, although the front page had gone for a mix of fraud rumours: "Is your MP taking a bung?" and mystery: "Where are they going? More homeless disappear from the streets…"

The only other occupants in the tearoom were an older couple discussing their somewhat disharmonious holiday plans. "It'll be fantastic, Sybil! Great weather, our favourite hotel, Christmas on the beach. Come on." He spread his arms wide, as if to paint a perfect picture of his vision.

Sybil snorted loudly. "With nobody I know apart from you? No grandchildren, Spanish flu, no doubt, and paella for Christmas lunch! No thank you, Charles."

"I'm sorry to interrupt but I'm hoping you can help me." I looked over at them hopefully.

Sybil snapped her thin lips together and glared at me. "I hope you're not asking for money."

I flushed. Not the friendliest of responses. "I wondered if you knew of any jobs going around here. I've just been made redundant. I'm happy to try anything," I rattled on, as Sybil's sparse lower lip curled up like frazzled bacon.

"I'm not sure why you think we would know of anything. We are pensioners, you know; charity begins at home." She rose from her seat and flounced out, followed a second later by an apologetic-looking Charles.

"Huh, she wouldn't know the first thing about charity." Prior to this, the matronly woman who always served me in the tearoom had maintained a vow of silence the Benedictine nuns would have approved of. "She's got a very high opinion of herself, that one. Leads poor Charles a dog's life." She shook her head regretfully. "He could have done so much better for himself. The most excitement he gets these days is being first to the newsagents for the morning paper!"

I pushed back my chair, gritting my teeth at the resulting screech of wood on concrete. "Well, I'd better be off and start searching on those job sites."

I nodded at her as she furiously wiped away at their vacant table and then stopped in the doorway as she announced: "If you're really that desperate, I might know someone who needs a cleaner. If you hang on, I'll find the details."

*

The oasthouse loomed up in front of me as I pushed the advert into my pocket. You couldn't really miss it, tucked away behind the main high street but impossible to ignore. I stared up at its impressive height.

"Are you coming in or just admiring my brickwork? I am a busy man, sweetheart."

Slimy didn't do him justice. Or shiny. He carried off both looks really well. His hair was plastered flat with oil; his jacket and trousers had a greasy hue that could really only have been earned by bathing in lard.

"I'm here about the cleaning job," I sort of shouted at him, having moved back from the overpowering scent of aftershave.

"Well, come in, sweetheart. I'm all for helping out the unfortunates." He gestured me inside with a flourish of a shiny sleeve. "As you can imagine, we've got lots of rooms and lots of stairs, but you look pretty fit to me."

Having finished my little tour, I had to agree with him about the stairs. "How often would you need me to clean? And how much can you pay me?" I asked, quite surprised at my bravery.

106

"Twice a week should do it. We have a lot of functions here, important people. How does £20 an hour grab you, six hours a week for now?" He leered at me. "See how you get on with it, and me."

"That sounds great, very generous, but I'm not looking for anything else if you know what I mean. I'm engaged to a lovely man."

"Well, bully for you, sweetheart. You're not my type either, but I do have some strict rules that I expect you to follow if you're going to work for me."

"He's quite weird," I told Rob later that day as I recounted my first venture into self-employment. "I think he fancies himself as – I don't know really, a bit of a ladies' man, a bit of a high-flying businessman."

"And what do you think he is?" Rob asked, expertly manipulating my toes.

"He actually comes across as a bit of a twit more than anything else, going on about not poking around in places that don't concern me, but for that he's paying me £20 an hour to clean and wash dishes, so it's all good." I yawned and stretched luxuriously. "You're so good at foot massages."

*

Two months of cleaning the oasthouse had seen the final days of summer replaced by fierce autumn winds and now the trees in the village stood naked, their golden leaves blanketing the ground in a crumpled mass through which I loved to scrunch. I'd paid out for proper cleaning equipment, added a couple of other regular cleaning clients and an occasional end-of-tenancy blitz and I felt like a professional. I hummed to myself as I loaded the industrial-sized dishwasher in the oasthouse kitchen with a mix of champagne flutes, pint glasses and nibble bowls. Three large recycling bins overflowed with empty beer, wine and spirit bottles.

"I'd like a word with you." His unexpected and silent appearances were always accompanied by an overwhelming stench of aftershave. Maybe he drank it or splashed it around the house like air freshener.

"Oh, hi Mr. Barker, you startled me appearing like that. You had quite a party here last night by the looks of it."

"Nothing you need to concern yourself with."

"Is everything okay?" I really wanted to ask him if he ever thought of taking his suits to the dry-cleaners.

"It's all peachy, sweetheart. I thought you might like another little job as you've been doing so well for us."

"I would love more work; I'm really enjoying my new life away from petty office politics."

"Well, good. You listen to what you're told and you obey instructions. That is what I like about you. Now, leave whatever you're doing there and follow me."

We marched down the quiet high street past tiny Georgian doorways surely intended for hobbit families; modest cottages with crooked chimneys sat comfortably beside more imposing whitewashed frontages. No uniformity of modern dull boxes in this village, rather a higgledy-piggledy hotch-potch of styles. We were approaching the beautiful, double-fronted house with the blue shutters I now knew as Pleasant View Cottage and I smiled at it longingly as we drew near. Then we actually stopped outside the solid wooden front door. As with all the other properties in the high street there was no front garden, but the entrance was surrounded by many pots of tulips, daffodils and crocuses. As Mr. Barker began pounding enthusiastically on the door I leant down to sniff and recoiled, realising they were nothing more than plastic fakes pushed into the pots of real earth.

"Aunt Rose!" Mr Barker was shouting through the letterbox now. "Come on, open up."

After what seemed like forever the front door opened slowly and the old lady I'd previously spoken to peered out, her face creasing with concern. 'Derek, I didn't know you were coming today. Are you planning another party already?"

"Auntie, you really need to wear your hearing aid. I've been banging on the door for ages. Everyone in the road's been out."

"Oh, don't fuss, Derek. The thing makes my ear hurt." She turned towards me. "Ooh, I know you, don't I? You're the one who said how lovely the cottage is."

Mr Barker, who I now knew was Derek, gestured for me to follow him in and I stood for the first time inside Pleasant View

Cottage. I tried to look around without appearing horribly nosy. Dr. Who fans would appreciate my immediate thought that it was bigger on the inside than I had expected. I tuned back into the conversation.

"Well, she's going to come round and help you with your cleaning and whatever it is you do. What do you say to that?" Derek nodded at his aunt. She looked at him blankly. "Cleaning! You're starting to look a bit shabby round the edges, Rose," he shouted. "Can't have people poking their noses in, can we? Thinking you can't cope, getting the council in? And put your bloody hearing aid in!" he muttered, rather like a rebellious child.

He began rummaging in one of the cupboards in the hallway, pulling out files and boxes and grunting with annoyance until finally he triumphantly produced two keys on a red spiral key ring.

"Look after this," he instructed me, peeling one off the fob and placing it in his pocket before dangling the fob and remaining key in front of me. "In fact, guard it with your life."

Rose frowned at her nephew. "Are you sure that's a good idea? I'm not one for strangers."

"I don't want to intrude if your aunt's not keen." I tried to keep my tone professional.

"Look, Polly understands my rules. We're onto a good thing here and you're living in the past, Aunt Rose, you've got to move with the times. All you've got to remember, Polly, is that no one is welcome in here without my permission and no one is allowed to poke about upstairs, not even you. You got that?"

"Err, yes of course," I responded, surprised by his sudden about turn on me.

"Well, can I have the other key back, please, Derek?" the old woman asked. "I do like to go out sometimes without waiting around for you."

"No Aunt Rose, I think it's best I keep hold of this so the whole road doesn't clock what's going on. I'll get you another one cut, if you behave yourself."

I cringed as Rose stalked off, leaving us standing in the hallway.

*

"So that's how I got another little job and saw inside Pleasant View Cottage," I recounted my strange morning to Rob.

"Sounds like he's not very nice to her," he commented.

"It's an odd relationship, actually. He seems more concerned with privacy and what the neighbours think than worrying about her. She's quite old and the heating was blasting away so she obviously feels the cold."

"Wonder what he's got to hide." Rob looked over at me as he filled the kettle to make tea.

*

My cleaning routine at PVC, as I'd begun to affectionately call the cottage, couldn't have been easier because Rose wasn't that keen for me to do much. She wasn't unfriendly exactly, but my visits made her tense and she took to following me about.

"There's very little I need you to do, dear," she often commented, and she was right, almost. The original Butler sink was sparkling and the kitchen units were clean, but old, very kitsch. However, I opened the oven and found myself peering into hell: baking tins caked with grease and burnt offerings, as my mum would have said.

"Ugh!" I shuddered. After tipping the loose lumps into the bin, I began to stack the whole lot into a bucket of boiling water and Fairy Liquid. "I guess it's not just her hearing that's going, poor lady."

The side room off the kitchen had at some point been converted into a bathroom and housed a simple white suite, which was fine, but the various stains on the pink carpet weren't a great look. The two rooms at the front of the house were full of character, with bare parquet flooring, intricate coving and ceiling roses. One housed a sofa, table and chairs, a TV; a small selection of photographs, encased in simple wooden frames, hung over the fireplace. The other room appeared to be where Rose slept, with heavy wooden furniture and an old-fashioned candlewick bedspread covering the bed.

"Do you not sleep upstairs, Rose?" I asked her one day.

"No, dear. Derek thinks it's safer for me down here. We've got a lot of dry rot upstairs."

110

"We could try and get that sorted out for you if you like. It's a shame you can't use the rooms up there."

"Oh no, Derek doesn't like anyone going upstairs. It's too dangerous." Rose walked off and out into the small back garden, signalling an end to our conversation.

Later that afternoon, after shouting goodbye and closing the front door, I saw the unforgettable Sybil walking quickly towards me, Charles following behind. "You're not actually working here?" Sybil asked, breathlessly, as they drew level.

"Hi!" I beamed at them. "Do you remember me from the café last summer? Yes, thanks for asking, I'm doing really well with my cleaning business." Already I could see Sybil's lip curling disdainfully as I pressed on. "Since we're chatting, could you tell me anything about the history of the cottage? It's still a beautiful house but it's a bit run down, which is such a shame."

"Well now, what can we tell you." Charles' moustache was almost standing to attention with excitement. "Back in the 30s it was owned by the Framlingham-Taylors, and in fact their family had, I believe, owned it for over a hundred years. Lovely family, the Framlingham-Taylors. He was big in textiles and had a hand in cigars. They had a rather wayward son, I seem to remember, and a daughter. Then in the late 50s the Framlinghams and the Taylors had rather a falling out and the place was sold off in a hurry." He turned to Sybil for confirmation. "It got turned into what one might call a commune, if I'm not mistaken."

"Yes, that's right. The things I could tell you!" Sybil pursed those now familiar lips. "The place was besieged with very odd characters chanting and moving about to weird bits of music at all times of the day and night."

"You mean dancing?" I helpfully suggested to Sybil.

"No, young lady, I do not mean dancing. Believe it or not, I was young once. I do know what dancing is and this was just a lot of shuffling about, peering through shafts of long hair and mumbling and wailing." She paused for breath before continuing. "And lots of visitors who should have known better than to associate with that sort of thing." She ground to a halt at this point and glared meaningfully at Charles, who looked anywhere but at his wife.

111

"What happened next?" I asked, wishing I had the courage to enquire if Charles had been involved.

The couple looked awkwardly at one another and back at me. "Can't really say after that. We had to downsize in the 80s. We're in the bungalows just outside the village so we're no longer in the immediate area."

I could sense Charles was in Sybil's bad books for daring to mention that they'd had to downsize, and as if by a hidden message they turned away. "Well, we must be off. It's been a pleasure." If Charles had been wearing a hat, he probably would have raised it.

I couldn't resist shouting, "Maybe I'll see you in the café sometime?"

Apart from an annoyed backward glance from Sybil there was no indication they had heard me.

*

That night in bed I dreamed about the Framlingham-Taylors, their happy lives suddenly torn apart by the family split and the sad need to sell the house. Rob surprisingly turned up in the middle of a chanting, howling group and began pushing aside their long hair and asking what they had to hide. I woke up in a sweat as the members of the group all began to look worryingly like Sybil. But what about Derek? What did he have to hide?

The next evening, full from a delicious takeaway, I outlined my thoughts to Rob. "There's something a bit weird about the whole thing. Upstairs is out of bounds and Derek is completely manic about privacy. Plus, there was also some sort of hippy commune set up when the house was sold in the 50s. I'd love to know what's really going on in there, but I need to get into PVC and have a look without them knowing."

"You know, you only call that place by its initials now; it's like a code! Although I do like the idea of you getting into PVC." He grinned at me and poked my leg lazily with his outstretched foot. "Do you think you're in a spy movie or something?"

"I do not! This is a real mystery. Why are they so weird and secretive? Anyway," I leaned over and kissed him, "I'm going to investigate. I just need a plan."

"I just know this is gonna end in tears," replied Rob.

My chance came a few weeks later when Rose informed me I wouldn't be needed for that weekend as she had to stay up at the oasthouse for a 'function'. I figured I'd be safe to get in and have a proper look around. I took the car as even I didn't fancy walking around late at night, plus it was absolutely freezing. I parked up by the cottage at 11pm and struggled to put my thicker jacket and scarf on in the tiny Fiat, cursing as I smacked my head on the steering wheel. Bundled up like an overstuffed penguin, I eventually heaved myself out of the car and stared anxiously at the cottage, which was dark and silent – but was I sure it was empty? I began to creep cautiously up the side path to make sure there were no lights on in the kitchen or bathroom.

"Oy you, what are you up to?"

Barely a few steps up the path I froze. Loath to turn around, I waddled about with as much dignity as I could summon and flapped my padded arms uselessly as a torch beam blinded me.

"PC Decker here. Can I ask what you are doing wandering about at this time of the night?"

"Errr…I'm looking for my cat, Boris. I thought I saw him on that wall. He's new to the area and he's not been done so he tends to wander off, looking for females."

"Hmm, rather like our beloved leader, I imagine. Do you have a description? Have you done a poster? What vet are you with?" I could feel a cold stream of sweat forming and trickling down my back at the barrage of questions.

"Uhm, he's black and white, fat, four legs, usual sort of thing and a vet… yes, I need to find a vet to get him done. I've been a bit short of money for that." Idiot, I cursed myself. Please don't let him take that gem to mean I'm a burglar.

He shook his head at me. "Shouldn't get pets if you can't afford them. Anyway, I'll keep an eye out for him, but I think you should just go home now. We have had reports of people hanging about around here, so if I can just have your contact details, I'll add this incident to the system."

"So now we have the police after us. Thanks, Polly," Rob scowled at me as I recounted my experience, my cold feet pressed onto his warm back.

"Oh, come on, what does it matter? We've done nothing wrong."

"Well, I haven't anyway," he mumbled, pulling the duvet over his head.

*

Two weeks later it was Derek, looking his usual greasy self, who gave me another opportunity to investigate.

"You might as well have the weekend off, sweetheart," he explained, handing over my wages. "Auntie will be staying over with me, helping me out with the guests."

It wasn't cold that Saturday night so I didn't need to dress up like an overstuffed Christmas turkey. I ran lightly down the stairs and grabbed the car keys out of the pot in our little kitchen.

"Where are you off to?" Rob asked, slouching on the kitchen worktop as he munched his way through a family size bag of crisps "Oh, don't tell me. Another attempt at breaking and entering." He nudged me and I swear I saw a wink.

"You know I have a key, so it's sort of okay. I'm going to the cottage and this time I'm actually going in to have a proper look around. I might be able to find out what Derek's up to or see if I can find out any more about the group who took it over."

"Well, god help that lot if no one's seen them for forty odd years! You could maybe bring an undertaker with you." He leaned over and kissed the tip of my nose "Just be careful. Don't get yourself arrested and don't forget your Mission Impossible outfit."

I parked a few houses away, confident that the cottage definitely was empty, and went in as quickly and quietly as I could this time; no hanging about waiting for policemen to spot me. Shielding the glare of my torch, I listened carefully, comforted by the thick and heavy silence, with just my breathing for company. The kitchen was partially bathed in moonlight, illuminating the gleaming Butler sink and the Aga, which now looked much cleaner thanks to my hard work. I walked through to the bathroom and smiled with professional pride at the sparkling basin and bath and the new sea green flooring. It hadn't been difficult to persuade Derek and Rose that the awful pink carpet had to go. I began fantasising about what it would be like to actually own the cottage and live here with Rob and I had just decided that yes, that would be perfect when I heard a sudden persistent tapping on the window of the room Rose slept in.

Completely freaked out and feeling like my stomach was dropping through the stone floor, I crept forward cautiously and saw Rob's face pressed up against the pane. "What are you doing?" I hissed at him. "Anyone could see you out there."

"I got worried about you. Came over on my bike to make sure you're okay. Can you let me in?"

"For goodness' sake!" I pulled the door handle, cringing as it squeaked open. "Come in quick. You frightened the life out of me, you idiot! You could have just come with me in the first place."

"I wanted to watch the rest of the snooker, but then I started to worry about you here all on your own. And look." He held up a Waitrose carrier bag.

"What, you brought the shopping with you?"

"No, I thought we might need some tools if we're going to investigate properly." He withdrew a grey metal toolbox from the bag. "And just in case your nosy copper was hanging about, I thought nothing says trustworthy more than Waitrose." He looked around "Well, this is pretty strange for a date night anyway."

"Shush, Rob. You've made enough noise to wake the whole road up."

"It's absolutely boiling in here, Polly. Can we open a window?"

'Of course we can't open a bloody window! Stop moaning. Why don't you go upstairs, see what you can find?"

Seriously wishing he hadn't come, I walked into the living room and for the first time paid proper attention to the collection of black and white photographs adorning the space above the fireplace. The glare of my torch highlighted the poignancy of a moment in time. Attractive people dancing and laughing, with long hair, short skirts and flared trousers. Was I looking at the start of a commune or just people enjoying themselves?

"Polly, Polly!" I was broken out of my musing by Rob's urgent hissing from upstairs.

"Coming! What's it like up there? These stairs are great, aren't they? Not too steep."

"Never mind about the beautiful stairs. I think I've found what your Derek is up to."

"He's not 'my' Derek and – where are you?"

"Followed my nose, didn't I? I'm in the loft. I left the ladder for you, but be careful, it's not fixed or anything."

"But I wanted to explore the rooms up here first," I complained, unwillingly climbing the ladder.

Rob grabbed my hand and hauled me through the hatch. "Look around you," he instructed.

A multitude of heaters were positioned all around the spacious loft, pumping out searing heat onto the thick mass of bright green leaves, the stalks soaring up towards the ceiling, flourishing under the blinding glare of huge lamps. Blackout curtains were taped to the single window.

"Ohh! So that's what she meant about Derek being a gardener."

"Seriously? Did you not get that? Especially since you've been working in this bloody hothouse for months!" I'd never seen Rob so incredulous.

"I wasn't even allowed upstairs to the bedrooms, never mind the loft, so how would I know? I just thought she felt the cold."

"Sometimes, Polly, you're too gullible for your own good." Rob began to wander around between the plants, fingering them experimentally. "Still, it's good strong stuff." He nodded approvingly. "I wonder how he keeps them so healthy up here." He bent down to check out the troughs and ran his fingers through the soil in a few of the containers. "Argh!" He suddenly scrabbled backwards, crablike, and shook his hands frantically, sending soil spraying across the floor.

"What have you done, Rob? Are you okay?"

He gave a shaky laugh. "I've figured out how he gets his plants looking so good."

Using a screwdriver from the tool box, Rob carefully moved some soil to reveal what was undeniably a solitary human finger enticingly poking up through the earth, a solid layer of soil clustered under the thick black nail.

"Oh nooo, Rob, that's disgusting! What's it doing there?" I couldn't resist asking. "Is there anything else?"

"Alright, twenty questions! What do you want, an autopsy?" He poked again in the earth, this time with a spatula-shaped tool. "Can't see anything else in this tub but there's enough pots up here so who knows. I really don't want to start digging around to find out."

I grimaced at Rob. "And you think that's why the plants are so healthy?"

"Shush!" Rob whispered suddenly.

We stared at each other, horrified, as the sound of heavy footsteps thudding on the ladder treads drew nearer.

"You just couldn't leave it alone, could you?" I pulled Rob back from the hatch as Derek's shiny head appeared in the opening. "I give you a good job and trusted you to take care of the old girl and you couldn't be happy with that."

"How did you know we'd be here?' I asked numbly, unable to think of any other response.

"I didn't. I came back to pick up some more supplies for my guests and the first thing I see is a bike propped up outside. Soon as I walked in the front door – which you left open, I might add – I could hear you two gabbing away discussing my private business, poking your nose in where it don't belong." Derek was now head and shoulders into the hatch, alarmingly, waving a gun at me. "You," he said, "are a nosy bloody interfering bint, and you," he turned the gun towards Rob, "are a spineless prat who can't keep a woman under control. Anyway, now you know the secret to my success you can be part of a new batch of my special tramp fertiliser."

He grinned gleefully as he started the final ascent into the loft. Suddenly, he began shaking violently from side to side, an unfamiliar look of confusion or even fear on his face. He grabbed desperately for a hold on the edge of the hatch before completely disappearing. A heavy thud and a metallic clang followed several seconds later. Finally, a prolonged groan reached us.

"What was that about?" I whispered. "What's going on down there?" We crept closer to the edge. I peered over and saw Derek lying motionless on the floor, one leg twisted under the displaced ladder. His Aunt Rose was leaning over him, now holding the gun.

She looked down at her unconscious nephew and kicked at him viciously. "I never should have let you worm your way in, shouting at me as if I'm an idiot, taking over. You're as bad as your father! He used to steal all my dolls when we were growing up, pull their arms and legs off and bury them."

"Err, hello Rose," I called down cautiously. "Are you okay?"

"Well, obviously not." She stared up at us. "Between your nosiness and my stupid nephew who thinks he's some sort of gangster you've left me with a real problem."

"Shall we come down?" I asked, more in hope than anything else. "Would that help?"

"No, I think for now I'll leave you up there. I have enough to deal with here." With that she turned the gun on Derek, who had been showing signs of waking, and shot him.

I gripped Rob's arm as we looked down on the scene unfolding.

A now fully awake Derek shrieked and grabbed at his left leg "What the hell did you do that for, you stupid cow?"

"If you're not careful I'll shoot you in the other leg as well." Rose shook her head. "You have no respect for me. You just think I'm an old woman."

"Well, you are!" Derek's face was scrunched up with pain. "Is that what this is about? I've been empire building here, and here you are just wheedling away at me in the background, moaning about keys… Owww!" He grabbed at his right leg as Rose shot him again.

"Building an empire? You think you're bloody Donald Trump, you do," she scoffed at him. "I didn't need you and your empire in the bloody loft. I was doing very well for myself, growing my plants in the back garden, experimenting with my recipes, drying the leaves to make my infusions and my cakes." She looked up at me peering down from the loft. "By the way, thank you. Since you cleaned the oven and my tins the customers say the flavour is even better, and so moist."

Derek groaned, but I couldn't tell whether it was more from the pain or annoyance at his aunt's lack of business acumen.

"You haven't got a clue how difficult it is out there in the real world," he said from his prone position.

"Listen, Derek." She kicked at his leg, careful to avoid the dark stain spreading across the floorboards. "Your father was a waster. When he got his hands on the family assets, he went through most of them like a dose of salts. My poor parents had to clear all his debts and I was left with almost nothing."

"You're the Framlingham-Taylor daughter!" I shouted. Rob grabbed me as my excitement at this sudden revelation took me dangerously near to the edge.

"Yes, I am," she confirmed. "You've probably seen the photos in my living room. I managed to raise money by encouraging people to stay here, get to know each other and have fun. Even the bank manager saw the attraction. The parties we had were legendary. It was a special time. Innocent." She smiled for a long moment, appearing lost in her thoughts, before finally shrugging her shoulders. "Then you turned up, Derek, with your bullying and your big ideas, your flashy guests every weekend that I have to come and wait on." She stood over him, casually holding the gun. "And then you start encouraging the local down and outs to hang around in my house." She giggled suddenly. "More fool them." Rose began marching slowly around the room waving the gun for emphasis. "Oh yes, homeless? Come in. You can sleep upstairs, no problem. I love to help out the unfortunates. The big 'I am'. You're a bonehead, Derek. You always were more Framlingham than Taylor."

"Shut up, Rose," Derek implored through pale clamped lips.

"Ooo, you don't know how long I've waited for this moment." Rose giggled again, her laughter growing in intensity to a loud cackling, as if she'd heard the funniest joke ever.

Rob nudged me away from the unfolding drama. "We've got to get out of here, Polly. She's totally off her trolley and he's bad, he's really bad." He pulled out his mobile, stared at it and groaned. "Completely dead." Shoving it back in his pocket, Rob glared angrily at me. "I don't suppose Miss Marple thought to even bring her phone with her?"

Ignoring Rob (I had forgotten my phone), I began ripping away the tape holding the blackout curtains to the window.

Pulling one of the huge containers over, I used it as leverage to pull myself up to the window ledge.

"No, wait, what are you doing?" Rob grabbed at me, almost succeeding in knocking us both over as the trough wobbled crazily. "You can't go out there. You could fall!"

"Rob, at least let me try. We can't stay in here, can we?" The pale grey bloom of morning light was growing steadily as I leaned as far as I could out of the opening. Then I felt my legs wobble. "It is quite high actually."

"Okay, okay, I've got you, but while you're there can you see if there's anyone about? Maybe wave a bit."

"What! What for? I'm not the Queen."

"And take these and chuck them off the roof." Rob thrust half a dozen long green stalks of cannabis plant at me. "Hopefully someone will notice and call the police."

I flung the cannabis stalks out of the window and followed up with some pliers and one of the screwdrivers (not that one) that Rob handed me from the tool box. A hammer and a set of goggles followed the same route out of the window, skittering down the roof tiles and landing with a clatter on the pavement below.

"What are you two up to?" Rose shouted from downstairs.

A sudden bang almost propelled me out of the window as a bullet sailed through the loft floor. Rob clumsily grabbed my legs. "This is getting worse and worse," he said. "How the hell are we going to get out of this nightmare?"

"I say, hello up there! You nearly hit me with those goggles."

I looked down to see Charles standing in the road, shielding his eyes from the watery early morning shafts of sunlight as he stared up at me, bemused. "Are you staging a rooftop protest? How jolly exciting. I love a protest, being a child of the sixties and all that."

"Listen, Charles, this is important. Call the police and an ambulance. Tell them Rose is downstairs, she has a gun and she's shot Derek, and she's very angry and mad," I added, probably unnecessarily.

"Errr, Roger and out." Charles almost fell over in his haste to get away.

"I just hope he doesn't let us down." Rob's comment coincided with another bullet through the loft floor that pinged into one of the containers, a large ceramic pot.

"You two better come down now so I can deal with you," Rose instructed coldly from downstairs as she replaced the lightweight aluminium ladder.

"I don't think we want to do that!" Rob shouted. "We're safer up here away from you."

"Are you sure about that?" Rose replied. "You might want to have another look around up there. You don't know what you might find."

"Oh, come on, I've already found some poor bloke's finger in the compost. What could be worse than that?"

"He keeps a snake up there." Again, Rose emitted that unnerving giggle.

"What?" I shuddered, looking around uncomfortably, suddenly seeing movement in every corner.

"Don't worry, Pol," Rob said. "UK snakes are not poisonous or anything. We'll be okay."

"It's called Kai." She smiled up at us with dead eyes. "It's a python. He's not eaten for a few days."

"She's bluffing, Polly," Rob whispered, grabbing my hand. I could feel his pulse beating wildly

as he clutched my fingers and then I could only hear a hiss, like a dog's low growling, as six feet of thick muscular snake slithered smoothly towards us, jaws agape.

"Kai the Py," Rose giggled "wants his human pie."

"Oh my god!" I shrieked, or Rob did, or we both did as we rushed for the loft hatch and half tumbled

down the ladder to land in a jumbled pile at Rose's feet, almost face to face with the still and silent Derek. We scrambled up hurriedly and edged away from the pool of blood to see the gun pointing at us, Rose having removed it from her apron pocket.

"Don't hurt us," Rob whimpered, almost from behind me I realised. My legs were trembling and I

groped for his hand to try and keep us both steady.

"It's a shame you had to interfere." Rose nodded at me, suddenly disturbingly affable. "You certainly helped me produce a better batch with your clean tins."

"Perhaps we can come to some sort of arrangement?" I suggested tentatively, noticing that a shadow had fallen across the sun rays on the floor.

She shook her head, suddenly engulfed in frustration and anguish. "No! You're as bad as Derek. I'm not having *you* ruining everything for me now."

I felt a glimmer of hope rise along with the sun: PC Decker's anxious face was peering, unseen by Rose, through the living room window. His shadow moved around on the sunny floor; I felt that any second Rose would see it. He appeared to be trying to signal something to me, hopefully that he wasn't the only officer out there.

All three of us were unexpectedly distracted by the appearance of the black and white cat I had seen previously. Tail high, he wandered boldly in from the kitchen, ignoring everyone, and sat to wash his face, paying great attention to each individual whisker. He then proceeded to thoroughly clean between each paw as we all stared, somehow hypnotised by this process. Satisfied, he stood and sauntered towards Rose, brushing himself affectionately around her legs, weaving tiny, graceful and intricate circles around her as she tried to move away from him. Suddenly he stopped between her legs and sat down, a fat solid immovable furry lump, back legs splayed out.

"Bloody thing, get out of my way!" Rose shouted.

Distracted, she waved the gun and I rushed wildly at her, pushing her to the floor as the weapon fired harmlessly into some wood panelling. Rose and I both sat stunned on the floor as police officers burst through both front and back doors, weapons raised as they shouted at poor Rob, the only person standing: "Get down on the ground!"

*

"So, were you really looking for your cat?" PC Decker asked later after we had been allowed to get up, Rose and Derek had been taken away and the RSPCA had captured Kai. "Because

122

until I saw that one, I'd started to think there wasn't actually a cat at all, and you'd lied to a member of the police."

I pulled a face. "Well, that's not entirely true. I did see that cat, but I just knew something wasn't right about this place, so I wanted to investigate. And I did have a key, so I wasn't breaking in, not really."

"Maybe you should think about joining the force if you're that keen," PC Decker suggested.

"Oh, god help us," I heard Rob mutter.

*

The next evening, I sat comfortably together with Rob on the sofa, the cat cuddled between us, purring loudly. "She was going to shoot you, wasn't she, darling puss cat? I couldn't have that."

"Shame we can't call her Boris, isn't it?" Rob smoothed his hand down her black and white fur.

"She deserves a better name than that." I smiled at him. "Listen, Rob, I've been thinking about my future and I think the police force might actually stifle my creativity, but I'm going to give it a go as a private investigator. What do you think?"

For once, Rob was lost for words.

THE PRESIDENT

By Richard Miller

It had been a long day for the new president. Earlier in the day he had been sworn in to take that role. For the latest holder of the post the date of the inauguration would go down in history as the day when he would start to make America great again. There were some who weren't sure when the good old US of A had stopped being great, but no one was going to argue with the commander-in-chief.

Since being elected – a result that surprised people both inside and outside the States – there had been a number of objections to both him and his proposals. Indeed, between the election and the swearing-in there had been a large number of protests that had shocked even the most experienced political commentators.

The latest person to hold the post first held by George Washington was in the Oval Office with his closest advisors; all were watching news coverage of the inauguration. The president turned to the press secretary. "Speak to the broadcasters and tell them that they shouldn't have edited the crowd scenes. I had more people at my swearing-in than were at my predecessor's. It doesn't make me look good."

"Sorry, Mr. President, but what if they say that the crowd was that size?"

"Who do you think the American public believes? Me or the media?" came the stern response.

The door to the Oval Office opened and the new incumbent's wife and other members of his family entered. One advisor turned to a colleague and whispered: "Will this room be big enough for all the president's family?"

The television was turned off and the conversation turned to discussing future plans and toasting the appointment of the new Head of the Free World; several glasses of wine had been drunk and many more would be consumed before the night was over.

The newly appointed leader joked: "Did you notice the seating arrangements for the ceremony? I enjoyed sitting attendees alongside those they didn't like or even loathed. The work of a genius, I don't mind saying, and I bet the sparks flew." His family and entourage laughed at the joke.

Towards eleven o'clock the president decided to call the meeting to an end. Tomorrow he had a long day ahead of him, including meetings with senior officials. He and his wife adjourned to their bedroom.

After entering the room, the First Lady took a bottle of single malt whisky from a cupboard. "Dear, a glass of whisky to toast today and the days ahead?" she said.

"Oh, you're being civil to me now? Makes a nice change given the stuff you've said to me recently. I guess you think that now I've been sworn in I still have to be nice to you and give you a few responsibilities. No chance. I can just about live with the nasty comments that you've made to me but having a fling with a member of staff takes the biscuit. Don't think I don't know. From now on our relationship will appear to be good... but behind the scenes? You can guess the rest. I just need to think of a way to end our marriage. A nice pay off should suffice."

"You think it's going to be as easy as that? You may have dirt on me but that's nothing compared to what I have on you. How is your secretary, by the way?"

Her husband's face reddened, and he was tempted to raise his hand. Instead, he muttered: "Give me that whisky. I need it." He drank the wonderful nectar in one swallow and looked at his wife. "Not having a whisky? Or don't you want to drink with me?"

"Not for me. I'll have a glass of gin instead."

The president strolled to the door. "Anyway, time for bed. You can sleep in the spare room. I would say I wish you a good night's sleep, but I'd be lying."

A few hours later the president stirred in his bed and looked at his watch. It was 6.30 a.m. He had not heard the alarm, which was unusual as he was a light sleeper. Something didn't feel right but he couldn't put his finger on it. He turned, expecting to see his wife, but remembered she had been demoted to the spare bedroom.

He ambled into her room and was going to say that they had best go to breakfast together, to at least give the impression that

125

they were happy in each other's company, but she wasn't there. "So, she's gone to breakfast by herself. That's nice."

The president rang his valet to assist him in getting dressed for the day ahead. No answer.. "Looks like I'll have to dress myself. I can't wait for him. Will have to get a new valet."

Staggering to the bathroom to have a shower, he felt giddy. "Too much alcohol. It doesn't usually have that effect on me. Maybe breakfast will perk me up."

After showering and dressing, the Leader of the Free World left his bedroom. Before heading to the dining area, he entered the room occupied by the Secret Service guards. "What the fuck? Where the hell are the guards? So much for them doing their job. Heads will roll. Wait until I speak to their boss."

He entered the dining area, which too was empty. For the next fifteen minutes the world's most powerful man wandered around the White House; not one person was in sight.

"What's going on? I can take a joke, but this is taking the piss. Don't tell me I've employed a load of Democrats. There are bound to be marines on guard duty outside; they would never leave their posts."

He opened the door to the outside; no guards. By this time, the president was feeling uneasy as well as angry. "Right, there are bound to be guards at the front gate." Approaching the main gate to Pennsylvania Avenue, he saw that there was no one there. Going through the exit, he looked left and right: there was not a soul in view.

With a start, he noticed that in the avenue there was a mixture of buildings dating from when Washington was built to the present day. It shook him. Then he saw the vehicles: they ranged from horse drawn carriages to modern cars. The unease he had felt earlier turned to something approaching terror. He was not the type of man to scream but was close to it when he observed four men heading towards him. They looked familiar and when they drew close, he recognised them with wide eyes as Abraham Lincoln, James Garfield, William McKinley and John Kennedy.

He held onto the wall. "I'm either drunk or dreaming. If it's a dream, why those four former presidents? I don't even like them. They are certainly not as great as me."

It suddenly hit him what the four had in common. In addition to being presidents, they had all been assassinated.

Kennedy strolled over. "Mr. President, we watched your inauguration yesterday." He held his arms out wide. "Welcome to our little group; join us. Oh, and by the way, if you haven't realised it already, you're dead."

I guess that would explain why I didn't feel well earlier, considered the latest occupant of the White House.

JFK continued: "We'll tell you who killed you, not that it will change matters, of course. You'll be shocked – or maybe not. To give you a clue, we have a similar record with womanising... although I don't think my Jackie was as bad as your wife. Follow us back into the White House. It's only fair to let you have one last look at the place before we go...elsewhere. What's the phrase? *'Out of the frying pan and into the fire'.*" He laughed. "It's been a while since the four of us have been in there and hopefully we can still find our way around."

*

Not long after, his valet knocked on the president's door. Receiving no reply, he entered the bedroom and discovered his boss lying on the bed; his body was cold. He tried to keep calm but could not help but scream and within moments two security guards came running.

One of them shouted to his colleague: "Get the chief-of-staff and the vice-president. And where the hell is the First Lady. Oh, and the doctor, while you're at it! It ain't going to help but at least we may know how he died. If he has been assassinated, we are for the fucking high jump."

PAVLOVA DAYS

By A.J.R. Kinchington

I call my days Pavlova Days when nothing goes my way. Attempts at the perfect dessert end in a sorry deflated sweet that reflects my mood.

*

The Mini was piled high with my things for the trip to the Isle of Stronseill, which lay off the west coast of Scotland. Admittedly, most of it was for Betty. Blankets, dog bed, tins of food and her comforter; a chewed up soft toy bear. The six-hundred-mile drive from London stretched out before me but that space of time would, I believed, help me decide where my future lay. I made several stops along the road for Betty and an overnight stay in a hotel. Refreshed, I continued and caught the car ferry to the island. The Atlantic Ocean was calm and deep turquoise while an exhilarating breeze tangled my blonde hair and put two pink spots of colour on my English complexion. It was around five p.m. that I arrived at the first shop and, I was to learn, the only one on the island. I had been told to collect the keys to the rented cottage from McNeil. The shop was more like a storage unit, with shelves groaning with flour, tins, jars, kites and boots.

'Are you McNeil?' I asked the tall man behind the counter.

'No miss, McNeil's awa' to sunny skies.' He snorted as though he disapproved.

'Oh, I'm here to...'

The man held up keys. 'Lexie will hae left messages at the hoose.' The smell of sausages cooking had Betty's tail thumping against my leg as she excitedly sniffed the air. 'Fine wee dug. Better keep the lead on, wild cats and heilin' coos roam free.'

'Are they dangerous?'

'Weel, let's say they're no' fond o' tourists.' He seemed to be enjoying the thought.

A young man, about my age, appeared from behind the door of the counter. 'Da, denner's aboot ready.' He smiled at me and, coming to my side, bent down and patted the excited Betty. 'Whit's my faither been sayin'? He a'ways teases new folk.'

'Thanks.' I sniffed as I lifted the keys.

'Pleasure. See you ower long. I'm Donny Fraser.'

Once outside, I resolved to visit the store infrequently.

*

The hills and lofty mountains cocooned the single lane road, the silence only broken by Betty panting in the back seat. Small rivulets of water danced down the hills, burnt orange gorse was interspersed with yellow flowers, dark purple heather clung to the land and Scots pines waved at me. A loch in the distance was surrounded by mountain grandeur and the spire of an ancient church was defiantly standing as tall as it could.

The cottage was as described, cosy with beautiful views. There was a note that said, "Miss Amelia Henshaw, welcome." It was next to a basket of vegetables and a small bottle of whisky, the island's own. I unpacked and made tea, but Betty was very unsettled.

'Are you missing Jack?' I said, picking her up. 'Me too.' It had only been four months since my relationship had ended, amicably, but painful none the less. 'He's off on his travels.' The words stuck in my throat. Betty looked forlorn. She was just a year old, a beautiful Springer Spaniel that was usually alert and curious. 'We'll be fine,' I told her. 'The fresh air and lovely walks will help.' We had three months to explore the island.

As the daylight gave way to a grey overcast sky, I thought it best to take Betty for a last walk. Outside, the cold air slapped my face, whilst the clouds spilt out their heavy burden of water. From seemingly nowhere the wings of the storm flapped furiously, giving a warning of worse to come.

Inside the cottage I took Betty off the lead, but the front door had not closed properly, and she bolted at a mighty thunder clap. I ran out after her, calling her name, but my voice was captured by the wind and lost forever. Desperate, I went to find a torch and spent an hour battling against the gale. Feeling sick with worry over the vision that old man Fraser had offered of wild cats, I wearily returned to the cottage to find a Jeep parked outside. Under a hat and an oilskin coat was Donny Fraser. I gestured to the cottage and we went inside.

'You're fair drookit, lass,' he said. Then, looking around, he asked, 'Where's the wee dug?'

'Her name's Betty and she's gone; I can't find her,' I said, tears of despair mingling with my rain-spattered face.

'Weel, she'll no' be far, sheltering if she's muckle sense. These storms blaw themselves oot afore lang. Warm yoursel' and we'll gang oot soon.'

He took charge, making tea and lighting a fire. We chatted a while and I learnt that he was home on leave from the army and in the last six weeks of his service. His billet was near Oxford, where my parents lived. His plans after demob were to join the family business running the whisky distillery.

'When do you think Mr. McNeil will be home?' I asked.

Looking at me sideways, he replied, 'No anytime soon. He's dead.'

'Your father implied that he'd gone abroad.'

'Aye.' Abruptly, he rose and, pulling on his coat, said, 'We can go noo, the storm's blawin itsel' oot.'

Although the rain and wind had abated the darkness was inky and ominous. Climbing up the wooded hillside at the back of the cottage took some effort and the beams from our torches seemed little help but were enough for us to eventually find Betty. She had lodged herself in a rabbit hole and her back leg had been caught in a strap attached to a small object wrapped in threadbare cloth. Picking them both up we hurried home to the warmth of the cottage. Betty was bathed and fed; Donny and I had hot drinks and he left with my grateful thanks.

Three days later Donny came to see how we both were after our ordeal. I assured him we were fine and thankful that the weather had redeemed itself by offering blue skies and beautiful sunsets.

'That object we found, it's a handbag. I found this inside.' I held up a stamped addressed envelope. 'It's to a Molly McPherson.' I read aloud.

2nd May 1971
'Dear Molly,
When you read this letter, I will be in Aberdeen. Pa has taken to the drink again. I am feart to stay here after whit happened.

He has forbade me to leave but I am goin' the night when it is dark. I'll no' be back for a whiley.

    Your best friend,

    Kirsty xx

    I will write to you but don't tell my Pa.'

Donny looked visibly shaken.

'What do you think it all means and who are Molly and Kirsty?'

'Molly and Kirsty are both eighteen and freends fay school. Kirsty's ma died, sudden like, and three months later Kirsty left. Her faither, Archie McNeil, was a dour man, not much liked by folk. Efter he died…' Donny paused as though he was going to add something but thought better of it. 'His sister-in-law Lexie took to mindin' this cottage. She tried to trace Kirsty efter her faither died but Kirsty never went to her grannie in Aberdeen and no one kens whit happened to her. Lexie had the polis lookin' an' posters for missing persons were put up in the islands and towns. Maybe Lexie…' He paused. 'She bides on the east side of the island at the distillery.'

Donny looked out of the window as though searching for answers. Betty broke the silence, which I had been reluctant to do.

'Let's get your lead and go for a wee dauner,' he said, stroking Betty's eager head.

Our walk took us down the hill to the little church that sat on the loch side.

'The kirk has been closed for a while. It's bonnie inside an' there's talk o' fixing it up for tourists. Mind you, it's the island's only one and folk hae to travel to the mainland if they want a bit o' religion.'

'Do you? I asked.

'No, not me.' He smiled at the thought. 'What aboot you?'

'Well, my father's a vicar so I guess I've had my fair share.'

We both laughed, an easy laugh that lifted our mood from the previous disturbing conversation.

'I'm back tae camp the 'morrow then five weeks to ma demob.'

I hesitated before asking, 'Will you come back here?'

'Aye, more reason to. I'll need tae keep ma een on you both.'

131

I felt a rush of pleasure at the prospect of his return and knew that Betty would be happy too.

*

In the days that followed, Betty and I took the mile walk to the church. It was easier to keep her on the lead as she was not yet obedient to my instructions. The autumn weather began its job of dressing the trees in gold and yellow. Deep, blood-orange bracken created swathes of rich colour so dense it took my breath away. I was falling in love with Scotland in more ways than one.

We ventured into the small walled cemetery where it was safe to let Betty run free. There were between eighty and a hundred graves, many with storm-worn, aged headstones. My attention was drawn to a few more recent ones and I stopped at one that had a white marble headstone.

The inscription read:

Moira Fraser McNeil
Born 1930 Died 1971
Beloved mother of Kirsty
R.I.P.

I wondered at the connection with Fraser and McNeil.

My thoughts were interrupted by the sound of a car outside the church. A woman was taking two black-and-white border collies out of the boot. Betty and I walked out to meet them.

'Hi! Lovely day for a walk.' She told her dogs to 'sit' and 'stay' and they were immediately compliant.

'Hi,' I replied. 'How do you do that? My dog doesn't understand my commands.'

'It's my job,' she said, smiling broadly. 'I have the stables and kennels up the hill. I'm Helen Grant.' Her familiar English accent was easy on my ears. I asked if she had lived here for a while. 'Yes, ten years but still I'm considered an incomer.' She smiled good-naturedly, and I warmed to her. 'I'm off round the loch, the dogs love the water. Would you like to join me?'

'Well, Betty isn't very well behaved; she has been quite unsettled since we came here.'

132

'She's young yet. Plenty time to train her; keep her on the lead for now. Where are you staying?'

I told her I was renting McNeil's cottage and she nodded slowly, her smile gone.

We started our walk and I asked her if she knew the McNeils. She was slow to answer and when she did, her voice had gone down an octave. 'They kept to themselves. After Moira died, Kirsty left. Not surprising really; her father kept them both away from social gatherings. After Archie McNeil died Kirsty couldn't be contacted. This is a close- knit community; no outsiders are told anything that doesn't concern them.'

'I noticed that on Moira's headstone she had a middle name Fraser. Unusual for a woman.'

'No, not in Scotland. Family names are often used.'

We walked back to the car and Helen continued to tell me about the McNeils and Frasers. The Frasers had owned the distillery for many years. There were three siblings. Moira had met Archie McNeil when he came from Aberdeen to work there. Alexander Fraser had chosen to build and run the store. Lexie married Angus Stewart.

'You know a lot about the families for an incomer,' I said.

'Well, I know about the family connections but not really about the people they are.'

'Donny didn't say he was Kirsty's cousin and Lexie was his aunt.'

'Like I said, no outsiders are told anything that doesn't concern them. If you stay long enough, you'll find that out yourself.'

The dogs were ready to leave and, as we headed back to the church, Helen invited me to visit the stables. 'Anytime you feel you need some company.'

I thanked her and headed back to the cottage. I was puzzled by this place and its people. Beautiful island that it was, it seemed to have dark secrets. I had never felt an outsider in my twenty-three years, and I didn't much like it.

*

The following weeks it rained non-stop. Clouds scudded across the sky like someone had pressed fast forward and when the wind howled down the chimney Betty cowered at my feet. Neither Betty or I slept well and at times the electricity had to be replaced by candlelight. These were definitely Pavlova Days.

When we could venture out again the earth was sodden and slippery. However, we took the road down to the church and Betty ran free in the cemetery. I watched her as she snuffled and scratched at the earth and was reminded of her spaniel instinct to flush and retrieve. It was when she started digging furiously by the grave of Moira McNeil that I had to stop her. The earth was soft, and it was with ease that she had dug a small hole. A silver chain and locket lay at her feet. She looked very pleased with herself. After covering up the hole we headed back to the cottage. The locket had the initial K etched on it and inside the locket were photographs of an older woman and a young girl. I assumed that they were of Moira and Kirsty and that maybe when Kirsty visited her mother's grave before she left the island, it had slipped off her neck.

Feeling that I needed to tell someone of my find, I went to see Helen at the stables. There were several horse stalls and I found her grooming a beautiful chestnut mare.

'Hi Amelia, pleased you came to see us. I am nearly finished with Ishbel. Come and we'll have some tea.'

'She's beautiful,' I said, stroking Ishbel's nose.

'Yes, she is. She is Kirsty's. We found her loose and wandering the day after Archie McNeil died.'

'How did he die?'

'Well, it was Ishbel that alerted a neighbour. Archie's car was found at the bottom of the cliff by the shore. They think he died on impact. Archie knew the roads well and it was good weather. It's all a bit of a mystery. His parents took him back to Aberdeen for burial. Kirsty must have left just before that. We are housing Ishbel for now.'

Helen led the way into her old farmhouse, which was cosy and warm. Photographs and trophies lined shelves and one in particular took my attention. 'That girl looks like this one,' I said, opening the silver locket.

Helen was wide-eyed. 'Where did you get that?'

'Betty unearthed it at the cemetery beside Moira McNeil's grave.'

134

'That is Kirsty's! She wore it all the time. She must be so upset to have lost it.'

Helen went on to say that Kirsty rode and competed in the local eventing competitions, but her father was never pleased for her. She kept her photographs and trophies with Helen.

'Why did Kirsty's father disapprove?' I asked.

'Archie was a pious man and he thought pride was a sin. He denied Kirsty any real freedom and she and Moira were not allowed to visit the mainland or the 'sin cities', as he called them. I think Kirsty came here to have time to be herself. She loved our horses and dogs and had a real knack of handling them. Molly used to come here too, and the girls had fun, like teenage girls should.'

'Did you ever hear from Kirsty?'

Helen shook her head. 'No. After her mother's accidental death I think she wanted to get away from Archie. He seemed to stifle her youthful exuberance.'

'What was the accident?'

'Moira fell in the yard at the back of the house. She hit her head and died instantly. The funeral was attended by all of us on the island. Kirsty will be eighteen now; wherever she is, I hope she is living a full life.'

We finished our tea and I was invited back to see the kennels and the new litter of puppies. Although Helen was twenty years my senior, we were developing a friendship that I hoped would be lasting.

*

The following day, I received a letter from my parents saying they were coming to visit for a few days. I knew why they were coming. It was to check up on me. I had left London in a pretty low mood and, as I hadn't felt inclined to write to them, they were worried about me.

I went to the store to collect groceries and was pleased to see that Donny was there. He seemed happy to see me and we arranged for him to visit.

I decided to attempt to make a Pavlova and dispel the negative attitude I had come to associate with it. After all, a Pavlova is to be enjoyed! As I took a cookery book from a shelf, I had no idea of the importance of my decision. Opening the page at the Pavlova recipe, I was astonished by what I saw. All around the edges and between the lines of the recipe was the smallest writing in pencil. I recognised the writing as Kirsty's. There were notes that appeared random at first reading but, as I turned the book around, I could see a pattern of thoughts and events. The writing was in a kind of shorthand:

No schl 4 days. Ishbel feart. Pa no' workin'. Ma sick. Kirk. Pa dram. Ma sick. No schl 5 dys. (This was written many times.) *A Lexi no' comin' noo. Pa dram. Kirk. Ma sk.* (As the spaces became fewer, the shorthand got shorter.)

Helen priz. Pa blazin'. M sk. MoLy me Aber.escap. 15y slv lock fra A Lexi. Padram Mafeart. Pa blazin' wi Ma. Ma died the day F71. Pdram. Funrl Ma no sk noo. getWrk. Aber. Greetin a dy. Padram. Aber.

I wondered at the life of the teenage Kirsty. It was what she didn't write that spoke volumes to me. It seemed after each "Pa dram" that "Ma sick" was written. School was missed and her longing to leave was apparent. In comparison, my experience as a teenager had been a happy one, with parents who were well and supportive of me. I had been free to make friends, engage in school life and music.

I also wondered why this page? This Pavlova recipe? Was it coincidence that during my Pavlova days, when I felt deflated and alone, it had also been felt by Kirsty? Even though I had been happy, 17 is an age of vulnerability and doubt. Yet I had support – which Kirsty had been denied. Miles and worlds apart, yet I felt a strange affinity with Kirsty. I wished so much that one day I would meet her.

*

When Donny came to visit, both Betty and I were pleased to see him, perhaps Betty more so than me. I had thought a lot about the culture of this island and the need to keep everything private. So, after chit- chat about his demob from the army and my time with Helen, I broached the subject of Kirsty warily. I showed him the locket and writing in the cookery book. He didn't say anything for a while.

When he did speak, it was to say with emotion, 'I had nay a clue it was that bad. I knew Archie liked a dram, bit nae notion that Moira was so sick.'

'It seems to me when Kirsty writes "Pa dram" that's when Moira gets sick. It's a pattern, isn't it?' Donny didn't answer, so I went on, 'The bag with the unsent letter, the locket and now this writing. Don't you think we need to tell someone?'

'Whit fir?'

'Maybe as her cousin you might like to tell your dad, her uncle. Your Aunt Lexie might want to know these things have been found. If she were my cousin I would want to know.'

'It'll jist stir it up all agin, and then whit?'

'I don't think it's your decision to make,' I said, irritated by his reluctance.

'You seem to hiv bin fishin' aboot the family. It's nane of yoor business.' Red in the face, he got up and slammed the door shut behind him.

I was taken aback but angry that once again he had shut me out. It was one thing not to disclose his family connections, but I felt that Kirsty's possessions were important finds. The pages she had written on were her story and had a right to be heard. I knew what I had to do.

The next day I drove up to the Fraser distillery and sought out Lexie. She was, I guessed, in her fifties, pretty, petite, and her smile was welcoming. I introduced myself and Betty and she was quick to shake my hand.

'Sorry no' to hiv bin to see you, busy wi' the still. Is the hoose ta yer likin'?'

'Oh yes, thank you, it's fine, though the weather has been so wet lately.'

'Aye, bit the dugs dinnae mind.'

Pleasantries over, I asked if we could have a talk and that I had some things to show her. She ushered me into her small office, which was set aside from the main buildings. I started by telling her the story of the night Betty got stuck in a hole during the gale, when Donny had helped me find her. I went on to tell her about the bag that had come out with her when Betty was rescued, the locket Betty had unearthed at the grave of Moira, and the cookery book. As I produced the bag, letter, locket and book, Lexie's eyes filled with tears.

'It's Kirsty's. I guid her this,' she said, her voice a whisper as she held the locket, tracing the initial and gazing at the small photographs inside. She handled the bag and letter with reverence and her tears turned to sobs as she read the notes.

I felt completely at a loss for what to say or do. I hadn't really thought about the impact they would make, especially as Donny's reaction had been so distant. Lexie was so shaken that it frightened me.

'Pair wee lass, we need to find her. Thank you for a' this, I'll tak it to someone I ken. It's no' been lang, only jist a year since I lost ma wee sister Moira.'

I heard Donny's words ringing in my ears. 'Stir it up again.' And I wished that I had never found these possessions of Kirsty's.

*

I was pleased to see my parents and even to answer the questions about my relationship ending with Jack. I explained that we had agreed that when he left for his travels it was best for him to go alone. We didn't hold the same view of our future together. Indeed, I wasn't sure where my future lay and that was why I felt it would be good to have a break from London.

My mother was quick to understand. 'Darling, you are only twenty-three. I know some of your peers have married but this is 1972; women are beginning to accept that we have other options. You will find your way.'

My father tended to agree with my mother on most things. He was a parish vicar and had heard most of life's up and downs. He turned his attention to the cottage and asked about its history. I gave him a brief account of what I had learnt of the McNeils and my finds.

'Something isn't good here,' he said. 'We need to clear the air.' He then went from room to room, opening windows wide and silently praying.

'What do you think it is?' I asked.

'I'm not sure, Amelia. I just feel uneasy. Go for a walk with your mother. I'll join you soon.'

As Mum and I walked, I told her that Betty and I had not settled since I came here. 'Do you think it's anything to do with Dad's feeling about the cottage?'

'Your father knows many things I don't understand, but he is usually right,' Mum said.

Dad came to join us but said nothing until we were back at the cottage, sitting in the warmth of the log fire and sipping whisky and coffee.

'Dad, how likely is it that with all the rabbit holes in the wood Betty would be in the one that had the handbag in? It seems there are so many coincidental finds all relating to Kirsty.'

'Coincidences maybe, but sometimes we are chosen to be the voice of someone who cannot speak for themselves. We can be a witness for another who has been denied a voice. Even if it is beyond our comprehension, only accept that you are the messenger; you don't need to know why. People regularly say it's being in the right place at the right time. I believe it is more than that.'

I looked at my father and saw a man who had an unshakeable faith in believing that we are but instrumental in a universal connectedness. I completely trusted his judgement.

We spent the week going for walks and driving round the island. We visited Helen and did a tour of the distillery. Lexie was nowhere to be found. When I asked where she might be, I was told she had gone to Aberdeen. I began to relax and felt much better being on my own when my parents left for home.

*

My visits to the store for supplies were few. On one occasion I saw Donny. We exchanged polite conversation but his friendliness was absent. To be truthful, after his outburst and accusations of me meddling in his family business, I wasn't keen to pursue contact with him.

I visited Helen and she gave me help training Betty. I was delighted that she asked me to ride out with her to exercise the horses. It had been a pleasure of mine when I lived in Oxford but London gave me little opportunity to ride. Betty loved to spend time with the other dogs and was becoming very good at obeying commands. Helen introduced me to some of the regular visitors to the stables, one of whom was Duncan, Lexie's son. He was about my age, tall, angular, with a ready shy smile. He increased his visits and Helen took to winking at me when he appeared. I was wary after Donny's performance.

The autumn was sliding into winter. Mountains were snow-capped and sent out bright sparks of light in the late sunshine. White-tailed eagles swept elegantly across the loch, snatching their meal with ease. Red deer came down from the hills and pine martens played in the last of the season's warmth. For all of old Fraser's warning, I never saw a wild cat and the Highland cattle were pretty and docile if not approached. This beautiful island was stealing my heart even if the men-folk were not. I felt at peace with myself and this land but it was soon to be broken.

*

One day, John Maitland, a no-nonsense detective inspector from Aberdeen, called at the cottage. He said he was here with his team trying to locate the whereabouts of Kirsty McNeil, following up an interview with her aunt Lexie Stewart.

'So, you haven't been able to trace her yet?' I asked.

'No, but in the light of new information we are concentrating on the island. I believe it was you who found some items that belonged to Kirsty.'

'Yes, well, it was actually Betty, my dog, that unearthed the locket. Do you think Kirsty could have changed her name, or maybe she doesn't want to be found?'

'Anything is possible, miss. We are exploring every avenue. We will need to take your fingerprints as you handled the items. Can you stay elsewhere for a few days? We need to search the cottage.' Maybe he had sensed the history of misery and tragedy in the place.

I went to Helen's for a week but neither she nor I speculated about what the police would find. She, like me, had her own private thoughts that neither of us wanted to voice.

A week went by. Tents were put up in the cemetery. When the news came, it was shocking.

Kirsty's body had been discovered in her mother's grave. Fingerprints on the locket were a match with her father's. His were on file in Aberdeen from when he had been arrested for a violent attack on a man in a pub. Pathology had proven that Kirsty had been strangled by her chain and wrapped in an oilskin coat, which also had her father's fingerprints.

When Lexie had gone to Aberdeen to see Archie's mother, she had produced a letter that she received after Archie died.

Dear Mum,
I'm so sorry for everything.
My lassies are in God's hands now.
Take care of you and Dad.
God Bless
Archie.

At the time it was not thought that it was a suicide note, but in the light of his accident and the discovery of Kirsty's body, it seemed more than likely.

The bag stuffed in the rabbit hole and unsent letter pointed to Kirsty's bid for freedom being thwarted when her father found her leaving at night.

What had happened that fateful night in the cottage was a story that had to be discovered. Why I had a hand in that discovery, I shall never know. My father had been right about the cottage and the bad feeling he had picked up and if, as he said, it was that I was the messenger then my job was done.

Kirsty was finally laid to rest beside her mother. A funeral was held and all the island people came together to mourn one of its own. How strange it was that, for all the secrecy within the community, they came together in shared grief. I believed this was a community with a warm heart.

On my last day at the cottage, I went to say goodbye to Helen. She sat me down and asked, 'Why are you going home? What for?'

'I don't really know. I've no job.'

'Well, you have here, if you want it. It's been so good to have you around. You are wonderful with the animals; they love you.'

'I'll be an incomer, won't I?'

'If Duncan has anything to do with it, not for long.' She smiled the broad smile I had grown to love. 'You know, Amelia, no matter where we go, we always come home.'

I made my way back to the cottage. The winter night was drawing close. The air was cold. Against a dark blue velvet sky, a thousand stars shone brightly, the mountains rising up to greet and honour them.

I made a perfect Pavlova. For me and Kirsty, the girl who, unwittingly, had guided me to my future.

We had both come home.

THE TWINS

By Glynne Covell

Ellie slammed down the boot of the car with brute force. Arms full of blankets and cushions, she stomped heavily over to the grassed picnic area. She was seething. This had been arranged for weeks with her friend Jenna from school. Ellie and her twin sister Sarah were meeting up with Jenna at this beauty spot as it would be a perfect place to celebrate the end of term. However, this morning, David from school had phoned and Sarah invited him and another lad, Andrew to join them. Didn't even ask Ellie. Typical. Ellie was just expected to follow. Agree with everything. No voice. No opinion. She would have preferred them to be on their own; she never enjoyed a crowd. It was bad enough with the prom looming on Saturday. Maybe she could feign a migraine for that? She was in no mood to socialise. She was not feeling at all well today but that was probably due to not having taken her anti-depressants since last weekend. She was determined, rightly or wrongly, to get off this damn medication. It didn't make her feel any better so why bother with it? She just wanted to be normal. Like Sarah. Unfortunately, she couldn't share this with her sister. Although Sarah was caring and sympathetic, she needed to do this on her own. Prove herself. Besides, she knew Sarah would worry and also involve their parents.

Both David and Andrew expected to get the right grades for Oxford while Jenna, with her love of animals, had secured a position at the veterinary clinic. The twins were destined finally to take separate paths. Sarah, a naturally high academic achiever, was hoping for Cambridge but Ellie, who struggled with exams and was not expecting fantastic grades, was not quite sure what she was going to do but pleased, at last, to be breaking away from Sarah rather than continuing to follow in her shadow.

A stiff breeze blew on the ridge, but it was a gloriously warm June day and the view from these cliffs was quite stunning. Looking out over the English Channel, the sea sparkled with sunlight while boats were plying their routes back and forth to the Continent.

Having parked the car, Sarah brought over the picnic hamper and placed it down on the large colourful Turkish rug. She redistributed the cushions around after Ellie had just dropped them on the grass.

'C'est magnifique,' she cried. Then, spotting Jenna approaching, she waved furiously to get her attention. 'Hey, Jenna! How you doing?'

'Hi Sarah, Ellie. Lovely day. I hear David and Andrew are joining us.'

Ellie nodded, miserably. In one way she was looking forward to seeing David, but she knew her infatuation with him was going absolutely nowhere. He was off to uni soon and anyway, it was becoming increasingly obvious that he and Sarah were getting close. Good looking, clever and great fun, he was always kind to Ellie, knowing how much she really suffered, being constantly in the shadow of her more attractive sister. Ellie was the plain one with a tendency to put on weight and who continuously struggled with her work and relationships. Sarah shone. Effortlessly. Tall, slim, with naturally blonde curly hair, an infectious laugh and a magnetism that always seemed to attract friends. Her natural academic abilities outshone most of her contemporaries.

'Ellie, don't judge yourself on what you see as negative points. We're all so different and believe me, you are such a special person,' David had said. 'Look at what you can do and never compare yourself with others, especially Sarah. Just because you are twins, you're completely different people.'

She treasured David's words, which he had said in a heart-to-heart recently when he had found Ellie weepy and struggling. His understanding comforted Ellie but the last thing she felt like today was watching the growing close friendship between her sister and the boy she so admired. What he didn't realise was that he was the only person Ellie had sincerely opened up to and now she had really fallen for him.

Trouble was, Sarah was kind and never condescending to Ellie but with every success her sister achieved, Ellie's self-confidence ebbed away a little more. She couldn't help

144

sometimes wondering if life would have been better for her if she had been an only child. It was as if Sarah had sucked out all the good abilities and beauty from her while they were still in the womb.

'Here they are,' shouted Sarah, jumping up and waving enthusiastically to the two friends, who were clambering out of a car parked next to hers.

'Hiya girls,' shouted David. 'Great spot. Let's get started. Open that wine. Non-alcoholic for the drivers, of course. They'll get their turn to drink on Saturday at the prom.'

'Hi,' called Andrew. 'Thanks for the invite.'

'Mind you, who needs wine today anyway with this setting? Just look at that view! The world's out there, guys, ready waiting for us,' cried Sarah as she twirled around.

David affectionately ruffled her long curly blonde hair and Sarah responded by placing her hand over his, looking up and smiling. Ellie flinched.

They all dropped down onto the rug whilst Ellie unpacked the food and David opened the wine. 'I've got some beers here, Andrew, if you prefer,' he announced, reaching into his backpack.

'Cheers, mate,' said Andrew, taking a can just as his mobile began to play the 1812 Overture. 'Hey, Josh, how you doing?' he said into the phone. 'Yeh, a few of us are up on High Ridge. Why don't you come by? Yeh, okay mate, see you in a bit. Good idea, grab some chips on your way.' He turned to the group. 'Josh is going to stop off. He's meeting up with some mates from his football team in town later to see a film.'

'Cool,' smiled Jenna. 'More the merrier.'

Sarah danced wildly round the cushions, clapping while everyone laughed at her high spirits. Ellie sat staring gloomily out to sea. She was not amused by this growing crowd. *It was meant to be three of us,* she thought. Having sliced up the quiche, she called out that the food was ready, eager to stop Sarah's exhibition.

David wrestled playfully with Andrew and then made a deliberate move to sit next to Sarah, rearranging some of the food and cushions to make room. Jenna poured the drinks and toasted the future.

'Well, we know this is going to be good if you made it, Ellie,' David commented as he took some quiche.

'Now, let's promise to keep in touch once we've moved away,' said Jenna. 'Thank God for WhatsApp. How on earth did our parents manage when they were young? Write letters, I guess. Can you imagine it? So formal. How on earth did they manage?'

'I know. Mum often says that when she was "courting" – there's a word for you – Dad used to write to her and ask if she'd like to go out dancing at the weekend,' said Andrew, laughing.

'Really? Amazing that it actually worked out. Didn't they have a phone?' asked Sarah.

'Nope! Not even one of those things attached to the wall. Hilarious.' They all laughed. 'Lived about four miles from each other and weren't at the same school so it was either write or pigeon post, I guess. What an age to grow up in.'

'Just one step on from the Victorians, if you ask me. Got to realise how lucky we all are to be millenniums,' agreed Jenna. 'We've got it made.'

'This quiche is definitely up to your high standard,' said David, winking at Ellie as he took another slice.

'Great,' acknowledged Ellie. *I'm good for some things*, she thought. She enjoyed cooking, but it seemed it was another one of her downfalls. She liked to try whatever she made but her diabetes required strict control. Her dark moods tempted her to comfort eat.

Andrew noticed Josh approaching from the car park and jumped up with open arms, ready to bearhug his friend in welcome.

'How you all doing?' asked Josh. 'School's out, eh?'

Ellie noticed that Josh had sat down directly opposite Sarah and, as so often happened with admirers, obviously found it hard to take his eyes from her. Being with Sarah socially was always very difficult but today, seeing David next to her sister somehow provoked even more feelings of hurt and resentment than usual; they rose to the surface and hung around her threateningly.

As the sun climbed higher, their hopes and aspirations for the future rose alongside it; they stood on the threshold of adulthood.

They were in high spirits. Apart from Ellie. She picked at her lunch, disinterested and bored with the happy company.

'Anyone want some chips?' asked Josh, deliberately leaning over to offer them to Sarah.

'Ooh, I can't resist chips,' she answered, smiling broadly at Josh.

Josh winked and continued to offer them around to the others. They chatted about the film that he was going to see and Sarah commented that she was desperate to see it too.

'Why don't you come with me?' ventured Josh, looking hopefully and directly at Sarah, with obvious intention.

David jumped in very quickly with the affirmation that he was going to ask Sarah if she wanted to go tomorrow, staking his claim. Josh nodded and raised his hand in apology. Sarah smiled warmly at David.

'Hey guys, it's going to be the first time that you sisters are going separate ways, isn't it?' asked Andrew. 'That's going to be strange for you.'

'Yep, first time for eighteen years. Big step for us, isn't it, Ellie?' said Sarah as she put an arm around her sister. 'We'll be facetiming every day though, so no problem,' she added.

'Sisters?' asked Josh. He stopped eating and looked confused. 'Who are the sisters?'

David pointed to Ellie and Sarah. 'Twins,' he explained.

'What?' exclaimed Josh, looking at one and then the other. 'Surely you're not twins? You never are!'

'Sure are. Known one another all our lives, haven't we, Ellie?' laughed Sarah.

Ellie nodded, attempting a smile to cover her embarrassment. Her heart pounded and she felt her face redden with shame.

'Unbelievable,' cried Josh, 'just unbelievable!' He looked from one to the other with an incredulous look on his face, not realising the irreparable damage he was inflicting on Ellie. 'You can normally see some likeness between brothers and sisters but you two...? Twins as well. That's amazing,' he added, pouring oil onto an already burning fire.

It seemed to Ellie that time stood still. She dug her nails painfully into the palm of her hand as if to ease this horrifying situation she found herself in. She so wished that she hadn't come and, once that thought escaped, she wished she didn't exist.

A long silence followed before David remarked that they were both pretty amazing girls actually, so obviously shared the same genes. Dear David. Trying to soothe. But it didn't stop Ellie from feeling completely wretched.

The conversation gradually lightened as they chatted about future plans, but Ellie did not join in. She could only think dark thoughts. No future plans.

'Hey, time to run, guys,' Josh said, 'if I'm going to meet the others and catch that film. It's good to meet you all. Good luck with those exams. See you at football training on Wednesday, Andrew.'

'Yep, see you Wednesday,' he answered. 'I guess we'll all be heading off soon.'

'Come on Ell, let's take the leftovers to the gulls,' said Sarah as she picked up the remains of the picnic.

Ellie nodded as she slowly got to her feet. They strolled quietly towards the clifftop where many gulls wheeled and turned in greedy expectation. As they walked, Ellie glanced back to see the others talking, heads together. *They pity me*, she thought sadly, tears filling her eyes and blurring her vision.

'Josh is nice,' commented Sarah, returning his wave from the car park.

Ellie nodded but did not smile. She recalled his comments and felt a new kind of worthlessness, different and greater than even she had thought possible. It was a glorious day, yet somehow the world seemed a dark, foreboding place. It was a tunnel, an endless depressing downward tunnel with no glimmer of light, no hope at its end. She resented her sister's effortless beauty and her achievements – although perhaps it was her own lack of hope that she resented most of all.

It took just one deliberate push from behind to unsteady Sarah. Then another for her to fall from the cliff edge. In that push was all Ellie's pent-up resentment and anger at her lot. A high-pitched scream filled the air, signalling the end of a beautiful day. Sarah struggled to regain her balance, arms flailing wildly and a look of horror on her face.

Ellie stood, numb, as if in another world, suddenly aware of the finality of what she had done. For a few moments a profound, glacial silence hung heavily around her and upon the clifftop.

In seconds, David and Andrew were shouting, screaming and running at speed. Ellie was motionless, standing alone at the cliff edge. Jenna bounded up to join them, crying hysterically.

'What happened? Sarah, Sarah…' screamed David, his face ashen.

Andrew was immediately on his phone calling for help. Ellie remained still, looking out to sea, watching the foam-flecked waves and listening to the pounding beat below.

'Quick! Help her,' cried David. 'Bloody hell, she's fallen onto that ledge but she's not moving. I'll go down to her.'

'No. Don't try it, David. Too dangerous! Help is coming,' cried Jenna, holding him back. She looked terrified. 'Ellie, what happened?' she whimpered, not having seen the dreadful act take place. 'Did she slip?'

Slowly, Ellie came out of her frozen stupor. Sarah was alive. She had not fallen to the rocky beach below. Looking down, she saw that she had been saved by a grassy ledge about fifteen feet below. Even the bizarre and twisted notion of removing her sister from her life hadn't worked.

In silence, numb and defeated, she slowly walked further along the clifftop and then to the edge. Without hesitation, she threw herself into the void.

A TALE OF TWO LOOTINGS

By Tony Ormerod

CADET JIM NOBLE

A woman, horribly injured, had crawled from the ruins of a house holding a baby under one arm, unable to speak but managing somehow to raise herself enough to offer up the child to him. He knew instinctively, despite his inexperience and even before he'd taken hold of the tiny girl, that both were beyond all help. Struggling to hold himself together, he was relieved and grateful when, out of nowhere, two St John's ambulance men arrived.

'Leave this to us, son,' the older of the two quietly demanded as the other, a much younger man, gently took hold of the ragged, bloodied bundle. 'We'll take over now.' Jim marvelled at their coolness, the calm, matter of fact way they handled themselves.

Police Cadet Jim Noble, patrolling a beat on his first day in the job, was experiencing the start of a harrowing, horrific morning. Nothing in his Buckinghamshire sheltered life had prepared him for that, despite the lecture given by Station Sergeant "Jock" Stewart on what to expect in the Blitz. The "all clear" siren had sounded hours before. It was 9 a.m. on Friday October 25th, 1940. There were no planes overhead but he still raised and shook his fist in a useless gesture towards the sky.

'Bastards, bloody bastards!' he yelled at the heavens, and then the tears started. Ashamed of his weakness, composing himself with difficulty, he finally muttered his apologies to the two men.

'No need to apologise to us, mate,' said the older man kindly. 'There's a mobile canteen around the corner … well, there was a couple of minutes ago. They're serving tea and you look like you need one. We'll see to these poor souls, trust us.' Grateful for their intervention, their consideration for him and their obvious professional manner, the young cadet merely nodded and thanked them.

When a siren had wailed its warning some hours previously, most people who occupied the flats and the few houses in that part of the West End had sought the sanctuary of a public air raid shelter but, inevitably, some could not, or would not. Continuing to patrol less than fifteen minutes later and walking slowly as instructed, lost in terrible thought and searching for any sort of drink, Jim was halted in his tracks as he turned into another seemingly quiet street. On the opposite pavement a house looked as though a giant hand had sliced it down the middle. The downstairs section had largely collapsed, reducing it to an unrecognisable heap of bricks and smashed furniture but, clearly visible, in the remains of upstairs, a bed was teetering on the shattered edge of a bedroom floor. Pathetically, wallpaper, its pattern comprised of tiny blue flowers on a white background, framed an intact fire grate.

There was movement. Someone was stooping over what, at first glance, looked like a heap of rags. Puzzled and curious, quickening his step, Jim recognised the unmistakable dark uniform of a helmeted ARP warden. Just short of reaching the scene, he was nevertheless able to see something that both horrified and appalled him. Startled, the warden wheeled around, fully revealing the remains of a dead woman. He was holding on to a knife.

'What in blazes do you think you're doing?' Jim, raging, soon found out. A glance at the corpse confirmed his suspicion that the warden was butchering a finger from a hand. 'Drop that knife!'

'Don't make such a fuss, friend,' wheedled the man, who was of medium height and looked to be in his late twenties. 'She don't mind, and the ring's worth plenty.'

'Just drop it. I shan't ask you again!' Jim was almost beside himself in his contempt and hatred for the man.

'Look, matey, let's do a deal. See what I've got here?' Reaching into his overall pocket with his left hand and producing an expensive-looking men's pocket watch, the warden casually held its chain and swung it back and forth. 'Like it?' he enquired slyly. 'This could be yours.' He still held the knife in his other hand.

When Sergeant Stewart had handed over a regulation truncheon it was made clear to the station's newest recruit that its use should be limited to extreme situations. Jim hesitated for a full two seconds before he reached into his belt. The sound of a knife clattering to the ground almost coincided with the high-pitched scream of agony as the weapon fractured the warden's right wrist. Not satisfied that he had fully made his point and sickened to his stomach by the nightmare of a morning not yet over, Jim stood over the swine who, on his knees, was holding his shattered wrist and cursing loudly. The truncheon was raised again.

'Cadet Noble.' A shout came from across the road. 'Stop it!'

Startled, but recognising the familiar broad Scots accent even before he turned around, Jim did as he was told.

STATION SERGEANT "JOCK" STEWART

A tough Scot and veteran of the Great War, Sergeant Stewart who, unreasonably, had a jaundiced opinion of Hendon College-trained, ex-university recruits, was beginning to have doubts about the wisdom of throwing Cadet Noble in at the deep end. He was not an ogre; his own son, a serving soldier in his old Scottish regiment, was about the same age, but desperate times had called for desperate measures. In peacetime, another experienced constable would normally have been assigned to hold a cadet's hand for a couple of weeks but, aside from the extra pressure of a war, there was a shortage of manpower.

About half an hour after he had seen Jim off the premises Jock's conscience forced him into a change of mind. After ensuring that the station was suitably covered, he donned his cape and peaked hat and left in a hurry. Having supplied the cadet with a map and strict instructions to follow it, but not too quickly, he was confident that catching up with the lad would be a formality. Knowing his patch, together with an encyclopaedic memory for the names and faces of many of the local people, good, bad and middling, had always served him well.

Ten minutes into the pursuit he spotted a familiar sight down a side street. Two members of the Women's Voluntary Service – he knew their faces but not their names – were busily engaged in handing over cups of tea and sandwiches from their mobile canteen to a handful of unfortunate people who, earlier, had emerged from an air raid shelter to find their homes totally destroyed or damaged. The fire brigade had been kept busy but smoke still billowed from several places and a double decker bus, upside down, sprawled grotesquely across a nearby main road. It was nothing short of a miracle, thought the sergeant, that the canteen had managed to get through. He also recognised two St. John's Ambulance men who, standing back from the small queue, were in conversation and sipping tea.

One of the young women behind the dropped counter paused and, nudging her co-volunteer, smiled and waved as he drew near. He had no wish to linger. 'Hello there, sarge!' shouted the redhead, employing the kind of cut glass English accent which, pre-war, would have curled the lip of the sergeant. In his eyes now, she and her kind were heroines.

'Good morning, lassies.' He doffed his cap extravagantly. 'Glad to see you this fine morning!' Despite their troubles, an elderly couple managed a smile.

'Fancy a cuppa?'

'Not now thanks.'

'It's on the hoose, sergeant,' offered the brunette, straight faced, as she waved an empty cup.

He had heard it all before, but he winked and responded. 'I ken that weel lassie, but just now I have to gang awa'.'

'Pardon?'

'I said, I know that but I'm in a hurry now.' He permitted himself a smile of his own as he turned to split away from the group.

'Have you got a minute?' It was the oldest of the two St. John's men who stepped forward and, with a friendly arm, prevented the sergeant from leaving. 'We think there's something you ought to know.' The ambulance men drew him away.

'What is it, Fred? I said I'm in a hurry.'

'The Met must be getting desperate, Jock, using bairns for men's work!' The man, a Northumbrian so almost a kinsman, spoke with feeling. 'We felt sorry for him, didn't we, Dave?' His colleague nodded in agreement.

'What are you talking about?' The sergeant, bristling, could hazard a guess but nevertheless he waited for an answer.

They provided him with the sad details of their meeting with Cadet Noble. 'We told him about this,' said Dave, nodding towards the canteen, 'but I think he was only half listening. He was in a bit of a state.'

'So were we, Jock,' a downcast Fred admitted. 'It's the sort of thing we never get used to, but that lad…'

'When was this?' demanded Jock, concerned, and even more anxious to catch up with the cadet.

The men both consulted their watches, but it was Dave who spoke. 'It can't be more than a quarter of an hour ago.' Fred concurred.

After thanking them both, the sergeant hurried away, determined to catch up with Jim. It did not take long. Within ten minutes the voice of the cadet, raised in anger, drew him swiftly to the junction of a main road and a side street. He witnessed, from exactly the same spot occupied by Jim only minutes before, what appeared to be an attack on an ARP warden. A blow was struck; a truncheon was raised for a second time.

'Cadet Noble. Stop it!' Moving quickly, he crossed over and snatched the truncheon away. 'What the hell do you think you're doing, laddie? Have you lost your mind?'

Savagely thrusting Jim aside, Jock crouched anxiously over the warden and offered his hand in assistance. In that instant his gaze fell upon a corpse. Stunned, puzzled, hardly believing his eyes, he looked into the warden's face.

'This bleedin' copper, look what he's done to me!'

Recovering his composure, Jim seized the initiative. 'See for yourself, sarge, look what this warden's done!' He pointed at the body and indicated a knife.

'Warden? If he's a warden my name's Rabbie Burns! Where did you get the uniform from, Charlie?' asked the sergeant, rising then nudging the whimpering, prostate man with his foot. 'Fell off the back of a lorry, did it?'

'He's broken my bleedin' arm!'

'You shut your trap or you'll get worse from me, I can promise you.' There was venom, a threat of actual bodily harm in Jock's voice. 'Stay put and don't move from this spot as I consult with my colleague.'

Ushering Jim to one side, the two men stood together.

Flattered that he had been referred to as a colleague by a superior officer, Jim was surprised when a reassuring arm was draped around his shoulder and the young cadet wondered what would happen next.

'I'm sorry I doubted you, son," Jock said. 'This nasty piece of work is well known to us. No one knows how he managed to dodge the call up into the forces and we're certain he's into all the fiddles, but we've never been able to prove anything. He's for the high jump now. Well done, Jim!'

'Son? Jim? – I can't believe this!' were the thoughts that sprang to Jim's mind.

The sergeant had not finished speaking. 'Listen, I know you've had a rough time of it from the off this morning so you must stop now. Go home. Relax. You've seen and done more than enough on your first day out – and well done again!'

Puzzled, it took a few seconds for the penny to drop for Jim. 'How do you know about what happened... and don't you need a hand here?'

'Never mind how, I just know, alright? Leave this to me. It's your first collar and I want your full report on my desk bright and early tomorrow morning. You acted in self defence; we agree, yes? If you think I need your assistance in formally charging this,' he waved a dismissive hand, 'this excuse for a man and then carting him off, I suggest you think again. Take a look at him and then look at me. I'm half hoping he'll try to escape so... See you tomorrow and get cleaned up!'

'Okay, sarge, you're the boss.' Jim turned to leave but was halted by an outstretched hand.

'Cadet Noble. I am – and it's Station Sergeant Stewart to you!'

For the first time that morning Jim managed a smile as he left the senior man to finish the job. Looking down at his soiled uniform, there could be no argument about its lack of fitness and now plenty of people would notice it. In fact, a small crowd had gathered from a safe distance away. Glancing at his watch and noting that the time was 10:30 a.m. he paused and, removing a brand-new pencil and notebook from the top pocket of his tunic, that fact was duly recorded. There would be plenty of time later to write a report, but he badly needed to get back to the lodgings to clean up and change into his "civvies". After that he would call in on a friend.

ELSIE

Elsie had realised that she was wishing for the moon. Something, wanted so badly, would never be hers; knowing that did not prevent her from dreaming that she could own it. The lovely maroon overcoat had occupied pride of place in one of the windows of the smart West London department store for what seemed an eternity. Standing in splendid isolation just around the corner from the main entrance, it was wrapped round the skinny contours of a mannequin whose facial expression, a mixture of aloofness and disdain, seemed to be saying: 'You can't afford this, can you, darling?'

Nineteen, blonde, slim and attractive, Elsie, who worked as a copy typist on a modest salary but was also hindered by a lack of clothing coupons, often sighed deeply. After all, as everyone reminded her, there was a war on! Why then bother about a new coat that she would never own? Despite everything, as she made her way to the office, having travelled by train from a comfortable, safe home in Kent, she paused every day for a few moments to check if it was still on view. Sure enough, nobody seemed to want it and there was no indication of the price. 'A classy joint,' she would say to herself as she continued on her journey. She was a great admirer of American film star tough guys; an adoring fan who worshipped them from the cheaper seats as often as she could afford the price of a ticket in her local cinema.

Her parents had said that the war would eventually involve everyone and so it had proved when Hitler unleashed his air force onto the capital. Although initially the East End docks were the primary target, the West End also suffered.

It was a life-changing moment when, on the Friday morning of October 25th, 1940, Elsie gingerly picked her way through occasional rubble determined, as always, to arrive for work well before 9 a.m. Needing to see the coat again and turning into the familiar corner, at first sight her worst fears were realised. Shattered plate glass littered the pavement but, as if by magic, somehow the coat – her coat – had survived. It lay on the shop floor, within reach, partially covered in dust. The snooty mannequin had vanished. Without stopping to think, the girl glanced quickly around, put one foot inside the store and, stooping, plucked the coat from the floor. Certain that she had not been observed, she thrust it under her arm and hurried away. But, as she regained the pavement, Elsie was under an illusion. Someone had seen her.

The office was only a few minutes' walk from the department store yet, to her relief, there was no sign of any bomb damage when she entered the large building that housed the four ground floor rooms rented by the employment agency that paid her salary. Arriving at 8:45 a.m. as was normal, and noting that no one was around save a cleaner, in a high state of anticipation and excitement she headed for the ladies' toilet. Once inside, after easily brushing away the superficial layer of dust and throwing off an old, well-worn gabardine mackintosh, the new coat was tried on.

A full-length mirror confirmed her suspicion that it was a perfect fit. 'I knew it, I knew it. It's made for me!'

The small typing pool was comprised of herself and three older, more experienced women whose typing skills exceeded hers. Nevertheless, and despite the fact that their salaries differed, they had respect and a liking for each other. On the other hand, they shared a dislike of their supervisor Miss Godwin, known informally as "The Dragon", a much older lady in her late fifties and one of the "old school" – severe, straight-backed and plain-looking – who sat in an adjoining office. Affording a clear view of the four subordinates, a large window enabled her to keep an eagle eye out for any slackness. Quick to identify and correct every error, her other duties sustained a belief that she was the "right hand man" of the two male partners of the firm who occupied the next room. That was where people either seeking or offering employment called in.

Despite the travel problems caused by the air raid, the other three typists turned up more or less on time and the morning dragged on for Elsie. Every now and then, unable to resist the impulse, she stopped typing to carefully open the deep bottom drawer of her desk in which the coat was stored. In her imagination she was back home, walking down the street, the envy of every other girl and woman in the neighbourhood. Sorely tempted, after careful thought Elsie resisted an urge to produce the prize for her colleagues' inspection. In the light of the discussion that occupied nearly all of their 11 o'clock ten-minute tea break, that proved to be a wise decision.

As was their custom, they gathered around a small table. 'Girls, did any of you see that article last night in The Standard?' asked Pat, the oldest, examining a biscuit that had enjoyed better days.

'I read The Star,' said Angela. 'But not often – it's all bad news!'

'My dad has it. I don't bother myself, but what was it about?' put in Joan, not noted for reading anything at all outside her office work. Elsie simply shook her head.

'I think I've got the paper in my bag here.' Pat put down her half-empty mug of tea and stretched down to the voluminous bag she carried into work every day. 'Yes, here it is. I'll read it to you!'

The article in question wasn't the leading story – that was usually reserved for the latest bad war news – but it was on the front page.

'Old Bailey latest cases, that's the headline,' explained Pat. Then, reading on, 'Shockingly, forty-five cases of looting were heard yesterday in the High Court.'

Elsie almost choked on her tea.

'Are you alright, dear?' asked a concerned Pat.

Angela slapped Elsie's back energetically. Coughing, struggling to regain her breath, a few seconds elapsed. 'Yes, thank you very much, it went down the wrong way!'

Pat continued to read the article. 'Disgusting, horrific, and contemptible were among the words used by an outraged judiciary, which, with no hesitation, handed down hefty fines and, in exceptional cases, prison terms.'

'My Bert,' offered Joan, wagging a finger, 'he's in the army of course. He told me he'd shoot the buggers on sight!'

Elsie gasped.

'Sorry about the language, sweetheart.' Joan stretched out a hand to the young girl by way of reinforcing the apology.

A loud knocking on the Dragon's window and an imperious waving hand curtailed any further discussion as they obediently returned to their desks.

'I've seen *The Wizard of Oz* a couple of times and I think we should be renaming the Dragon,' whispered Pat. 'Don't you think she's the spitting image of the Wicked Witch of the West?' Everyone except Elsie giggled.

BOB BROWN

Bob Brown had spent most of the morning cleaning up his father's department store in the wake of the overnight air raid. No easy task given that his leg had been giving trouble, forcing him into sitting down occasionally to ease the pain. Grateful for the cheerful help given by two of the senior female assistants, who had no objection to dirtying their hands, and blissfully unaware of their undying devotion towards him, he considered that working together, with others, they had made opening up a formality. Arrangements to board up shattered windows with a local trader were in hand and Bob was satisfied that the premises could be made secure before closing time. They had been lucky.

'Oh Bob, there's no sign of that special maroon coat in the side window. The mannequin must be somewhere around.'

'Thank you, Brenda. Actually, I already know, but thanks again and well spotted!'

'But surely how…?'

'Brenda, I've got more on my mind right now!' Bob interrupted in an unusually abrupt manner. 'For a start, we will be opening in five minutes.' He looked up at the large wall clock which, like most things, had fortunately survived the raid. 'Just tell the rest of the staff on this floor, please, and ask Janet to alert everyone upstairs. We open at one o'clock on the dot!'

Only twenty-two, Bob considered himself a very fortunate young man. The medics at Dunkirk, working in horrendous conditions, had saved his life. Safely transported home, he had endured two painful operations on a right leg which, at first sight, according to the top Harley Street surgeon, would have to be amputated. Thanks to some excellent work, that life-changing procedure had not been necessary. Second Lieutenant Brown had left a South London hospital with a limp that would never completely leave him, a Military Cross and the knowledge that he could never fight for his country again.

*

At the same time that Bob's department store opened, Elsie turned down an invitation to join the other typists for their usual lunchtime meal in the local Lyons Corner House restaurant. Desperately needing time to think, she made the excuse that she had hardly any money on her.

'Don't worry about that, love, it's my treat,' offered the ever-generous Pat. 'Come on, it's no fun without you!'

The others laughed. Elsie forced a thin smile. 'No thanks, Pat. You lot go on; I'm not hungry in any case and I can catch up with my reading.' She produced the latest copy of *The Picturegoer* from her desk drawer.

'Don't tell me, it's Errol Flynn on the cover?' suggested Angela.

'Probably Clark Gable,' said Joan confidently.

'Or what about Cary Grant?' asked Pat triumphantly, before adding, 'Perhaps not, he's not tough enough for our Elsie!'

'Be off with you!' said Elsie. 'It's none of those. Have a good lunch and I'll see you later.'

'Probably spam and chips again, eh girls? Are you feeling alright, Elsie? Only you're looking a bit down.'

'Pat,' thought Elsie. 'Always mothering me!' There were plenty of things to be down about. How and when was it all going to end?

Finally alone, Elsie spent a few minutes halfheartedly rifling through the pages of her magazine. After reading a few sentences, lacking concentration, she threw it aside. The girl could not go on fooling herself; something had to be done about the coat.

Aside from her lovely co-workers – they would never believe that she could afford to buy it – what about her honest, hard-working parents? There would be no way that she could explain away such an expensive item. In particular, Dad was always going on about "spivs" and crooks who dealt in luxury goods that had "fallen off the back of a lorry", which no decent girl should ever get involved with. Of course, his "little girl" could do no wrong. Now thinking it through she knew she had been impetuous but, worse than that, she was a looter. A thief! Her mind was made up. Whatever the consequences, no matter how difficult, the stolen property would have to be returned.

*

Cadet Jim's landlady Gladys, a widow in her sixties, was out when, at half past eleven, he returned to his lodgings in Lewisham. She usually fussed over him. Changing into casual clothes after bathing, having discarded the soiled uniform, he imagined that, at the very least, she would offer to sponge it clean. In a short while they had managed to bond but he was, in this instance, overly optimistic.

It had been an eye-opening morning but soon, he told himself as he boarded a train at Lewisham station, there would be an opportunity to unburden himself onto someone who had always listened; someone who had gone through a worse hell. Firm friends, even before their pre-war university days at Cambridge, they had chosen different career paths. Leaving Charing Cross station in the early afternoon sun and walking quickly the mile or so towards his destination, Jim noted that bombs meant for the Docklands had, like those on his beat, demolished or damaged some properties whilst others, ostensibly, seemed untouched. Smoke was still rising from some of the rubble. Skirting around the roads and streets he patrolled in the morning, he was greatly troubled; fearful of what the future held for himself, his friends and family and, most of all, his country. It was only the beginning of something dreadful. That was a certainty.

Men were busily engaged in boarding up windows as he approached the store but his eyes were drawn to a large piece of cardboard that had been nailed onto one of the massive front entrance doors. Handwritten, bravely defiant, it proclaimed: 'OPEN FOR BUSINESS AS USUAL.'

Briefly lifted from his melancholy, Jim suddenly realised that, like a fool, he had not bothered to check whether his friend would be on the premises today. Once inside, he sought the help of one of the lady assistants. 'Excuse me Miss, is Bob Brown around?'

When Jim was shown into Bob's office the assistant was

161

taken aback by the intense reaction of the two men. There was a great deal of vigorous hand shaking, back slapping, and cries of 'How are you?' The visitor had said that he wanted to surprise her boss and there was no doubt about that; were they brothers? She smiled, content to simply slip away and leave them to it.

When Bob asked Jim if he would like a drink it was only a matter of seconds before they were both sipping large whisky and sodas. After enquiring after each other's families, the conversation switched to the war, and in particular, the recently concluded Battle of Britain.

'Thank God for the RAF!' exclaimed Bob, raising his glass in salute.

'Amen to that,' added Jim. Then, draining his glass, he said, 'Let's have another. I'm in need of several!' They fell silent as they topped up their glasses.

Bob was alarmed by the way his friend was attacking his drink and wondered why he was out of uniform. Sensing something was wrong, he asked if Jim was still in the Met.

'Well, Bob, yes of course. You're wondering why I'm out of uniform?'

'I suppose I am, but – are you on leave?'

'No, no.' There was a short pause as he greedily drained his glass, which was promptly thrust forward again. 'I've got the afternoon off, so I suppose I'm not on duty. Any chance of another, pal? Make it neat.'

'What's the matter, Jim? Sit down before you fall down.' Bob, concerned, guided his friend towards a large comfortable armchair and pushed him into it. 'You look all in and you never could take your drink, could you? When did you last eat?'

'Do you know, I can't remember. Must have been early this morning? That's right! Gladys, she cooked breakfast for me – and I think I'm going to be sick.'

Wondering who Gladys was but more concerned for his brand-new carpet, Bob lost no time in leading Jim out of the door and into the gents', which, fortunately, if only temporarily, was only a few yards away and empty of customers.

'Come back when you're finished and cleaned up and I'll rustle up some coffee and sandwiches, okay? Bloody hell,' he suppressed a laugh, 'it's Cambridge all over again!' There was a muffled acknowledgment from one of the cubicles.

Twenty minutes later, a more composed Cadet Noble, after three mugs of black coffee and suitably chastened, sat opposite his best friend. Nibbling on one of the offered sandwiches he found that his appetite had deserted him. When asked 'Tell me, what's happened today?' he was ashamed of himself and on reflection, conscious that his hectic morning paled into insignificance next to the horrors endured by Bob back in June.

Trying to change the subject, he asked a question. 'How's your leg now?'

'Getting better slowly, thanks, but I've run my last marathon.'

'I didn't know you were a runner!'

'I'm joking, you clot! Look, I'm worried. Never mind my leg! Are you in trouble? And if so, how can I help?'

Jim needed to talk; that was the best, the only way he could be helped. He started from the beginning.

His graphic account of the encounter with a dying woman, her dead baby and the kindness of the two St. John's men who had come to the rescue found him reliving the episode, which very nearly unmanned him again. Although full of compassion for his friend, it also brought back to Bob's mind his own private demons of Dunkirk, which still haunted him at night when sleep was impossible.

When Jim related the other event, concerning the unspeakable swine who mutilated a corpse in an effort to steal a ring, Bob, shocked, seemed curiously interested in the crime of looting. They agreed that the man concerned should be thrown into prison for a very long time, but he asked if, in Jim's opinion, there were degrees of looting. For example, if no one was hurt. Was the value of anything looted taken into account and what about the age and sex of the looter? The new recruit, Jim had not yet given the matter any thought but he said that, with more experience, an answer would be forthcoming.

'There's no one quite like Bob,' thought Jim as he made his way back to Charing Cross. One hour with him had boosted his flagging self-confidence. More importantly, it had reignited a resolution to stay in the Met; to make progress in police work, like his father before him. 'A baptism of fire' and, regarding Sergeant Stewart, 'an old hand whose bark is worse than his bite' were two of the phrases employed by his friend. A tough beginning that had earned a heartfelt 'well done' from the sergeant also meant a lot. Uncertain of what the immediate future held for him – more intense Nazi air raids, more fraught mornings, more tragic deaths? – Jim nevertheless felt a better man for his first experience of it.

Bob's interest in the looting case was a surprise but he dismissed it from his mind. Striding out despite a woozy head and noting from his watch that it was two thirty p.m. he reminded himself that he owed his sergeant a written report.

*

Pat, Angela and Joan had spent some of their lunch break in the restaurant making sarcastic but, to their minds, witty comments concerning the amount and quality of their meals. Pat had been wrong. The main course was not spam and chips; it was rissoles and chips.

'Makes a change,' said Angela, sniffing.

'But not by much,' added Joan.

It was the sort of exchange that kept the three women – and Elsie, normally with them – entertained at a difficult time and some, although not all, of the many female waiting staff enjoyed their banter. The expression 'Don't you know there's a war on?', which often came into play, had become a little frayed around the edges with use. The trio did not need to be reminded, preferring instead any other subject under the sun.

'I'm worried about Elsie, she's such a love.' Pat, the leader as usual, raised another topic. 'It's not like her to refuse food and she seems so... I don't know, so withdrawn today. Is she unwell, do you think?'

'Boyfriend trouble, perhaps?' suggested Angela.

There was a short pause. 'No, I don't think she has one,' said Joan after giving it some thought. 'But if she has, she's kept quiet about it and Errol Flynn's spoken for!'

'When we get back, I'll find out,' promised Pat.

Her two friends shared a doubtful look that suggested minding their own business would be the best option, but they refrained from saying so.

None of them needed to worry. At two o'clock they were back

in the office where Elsie seemed to be in a much happier mood. Having made up her mind about returning the coat their young friend, although still grappling mentally with the how and when and not totally confident of a satisfactory outcome, nevertheless felt that it was the right thing to do.

All her hopes seemed to evaporate half an hour later.

It was Joan who glanced towards the Dragon's window and stopped typing. 'I say, girls, that's a policewoman, isn't it?'

There was no mistaking the familiar blue uniform, complete with an unflattering hat. All typing stopped.

'I wonder what she wants?' said Pat, her curiosity aroused.

Elsie knew. Mumbling a hardly audible 'Excuse me,' she almost ran towards the ladies'. Once inside, she caught sight of herself in the mirror; the same full-length mirror which a young girl had excitedly, triumphantly used to flaunt herself only a few hours earlier, was now showing an image of despair. It would be impossible to explain away her behaviour. No way back by telling the police that the coat would soon be returned. What would people think of her? Caught red-handed, branded a criminal, ostracised by society. Would she go to prison? Minutes passed.

When the door opened, Elsie was on the verge of hysteria. It was Pat. 'Elsie, you're wanted.'

'I know. Give me a second, please.'

Elsie's last thoughts, as she braced herself to re-enter the typing room, were for her heartbroken parents who would have to come to terms with the knowledge that their daughter was a criminal. Her colleagues, who would soon be regarding her with contempt, one of the partners and the policewoman, who seemed to be staring at her in an aggressive manner, were gathered. Standing together. Waiting.

'This lady has brought us bad news,' began the boss, nodding at the WPC and then turning towards Elsie. 'I'm sorry to tell you that your supervisor's parents were killed in the air raid last night.'

Everyone glanced towards the window. The Dragon was slumped over her desk, head in hands.

Elsie was the first to react. "Oh my God, oh my God!" Almost keeling over, she began to sob uncontrollably and loudly. As if that was infectious, Pat, Angela and Joan followed suit, closely followed by the policewoman who, new to the job, had been tasked to deliver the information. In Elsie's case her tears were of relief; something which she, to her credit, privately regretted later.

Even the boss was affected. 'There, there, ladies, don't cry,' he said. Then, handing Pat his handkerchief, 'I know you're all very fond of Lavinia!'

Stunned, Pat stopped weeping, partially wiped her face and reflected on the fact that none of them had known Miss Godwin's Christian name. Less surprising was the assumption that the bloke's "right hand man" was actually liked by her underlings. Typical of a bloody male who was waited on hand and foot. What did he know? She too, but later, regretted her callous thoughts.

'Yes, sir, of course, sir,' on consideration, seemed the appropriate response.

The policewoman was thanked and gladly left the building whereupon, at three o'clock, as a mark of respect, everyone was given the rest of the day off.

*

Bob was amazed by the number of customers that had come through the doors of his father's store. They had queued to get in. There were many regulars among them who seemed anxious to show their support for his dad, a man who, over the long years, had provided them with value for money on a wide range of goods. The policy of positioning the department store's pricing competitively between those of Woolworths and Marks and Spencer had been a sound business decision. Opting for service in the army just before the war, against his father's wishes, had finally led to Bob's life-threatening wounds suffered at Dunkirk. It was then a choice between a desk job with the military and working for his father and, after choosing the latter option, he was surprised how much he was enjoying the challenge. All this, amongst other unrelated things, were churning over and over in his mind as he toured around the store, pausing every now and then for a quick word with one of the predominately female staff and, where appropriate, offering a thank you for turning up to work in such turbulent times.

Choosing to take the stairs rather than the lift in order to exercise his leg, he found it hard going and not a little painful, but he was ever mindful of the doctor's advice. Standing at a large window that had survived the blast, the view from the upper floor gave him some idea of the extent of the damage caused by the raid. Some buildings, those closest to the store, seemed to have been spared the worst of it whilst others, also close by, had taken a pounding. Bob could not help but wonder how long into the future the store would survive intact as his gaze shifted downwards to the pavement immediately in front of the main entrance. It was gratifying to note that customers continued to stream in.

Something else was occupying his mind. How often had he mocked the very idea of falling in love at first sight? Before the war, meeting up with a few young attractive girls at the tennis club had been a purely temporary diversion. There was plenty of time, he had told himself (and his parents), before he would feel any need to settle down. In any case, the army was a priority for him. He was not a shy person, nor was he an impulsive one.

He thought of her as "the girl with the pretty face and the long blonde hair" who, transfixed, seemingly hypnotised by the coat on display in one of the windows, had not even noticed him standing to one side in the background. She had caught his eye on more than one occasion but he had done nothing about it; not even when, this morning, she had lifted the coat off the floor and hurried away. Conviction that, with an injured leg, he could never have intercepted the girl, coupled with the fact that he was inexplicably, incredibly in love with her, had clouded his judgement. Glancing down again, he saw something that both surprised and excited him. Surely he was not mistaken? Turning abruptly, and painfully, he hurried to the lift.

*

After waiting patiently for the other typists to leave the office, Elsie looked for and then found (in Pat's desk!) a large enough carrier bag to transport the coat. Once outside, she was surprised to see how crowded the streets had become; it almost felt like peacetime – if she ignored some shattered buildings. Sadly, a few business premises had not reopened.

The problem of returning the stolen item without causing at the very least awkward questions which would have to be answered was exercising her mind as she walked towards the store. In her charming naivety, it never crossed her mind that, safely under a cloak of anonymity, it could be sent by post. Reaching the main entrance and pausing, having very nearly lost her nerve, she briefly raised her head as if seeking inspiration, took a deep breath and propelled herself forward through the doors.

It was not a first visit. In the past, during a couple of lunchtime breaks, Elsie had made modest purchases and then circulated in admiration around all the good things displayed. She may have been unable to afford them but she had a good idea of where everything was. Deciding that the information desk would be the best, most appropriate place to start she headed in that direction.

A very young girl was on duty. Just sixteen, a recent recruit straight from school, she was anxious to make an impression. 'Good afternoon, Madam, how can I help you?'

Taken aback – no one ever called her Madam; she wasn't that old, was she? – Elsie was distracted for a moment or two but, rallying, she placed the carrier bag on the counter and prepared herself for surrender. Before she could utter a word, they were interrupted.

'Miss Jones, kindly leave this to me.' It was a young man who, not unkindly, assumed command by opening the flap at the side of the counter before gently ushering the young girl out and taking her position.

'Of course, sir. I'll go then, shall I, sir?' the girl hesitated, unsure.

'If you wouldn't mind? Thank you, Miss Jones.'

The assistant smiled prettily at her boss and departed.

'Hello there,' said the man, grinning broadly. Elsie thought he reminded her of a slightly younger Errol Flynn, even down to the thin moustache. The way he was looking at her was disconcerting. 'Can I help you?' he enquired.

After rehearsing her lines over and over in her head, somehow, under his admiring gaze, she did not know where to start. Finally, she found her courage. 'I found this coat.' She produced it bravely with a flourish. 'I think it's yours.' It sounded lame but it was the best version of events she could come up with.

'Really? I don't think so, dear. It's not my colour.'

'I mean, I mean...'

'Sorry, I'm pulling your leg! I saw you this morning. You were taking it on approval – correct?'

Not for the first time today, Elsie gasped. This was not happening! 'Why didn't you stop me?'

'I have no rational explanation. What's your name, by the way? Mine's Bob.'

'I'm Elsie.'

'Well, Elsie, you don't know me, but I feel that I know you because I've seen you window shopping outside off and on for ages. Tell me, why did you bring this coat back? Is it because you're as nice as you look?'

Her blush almost matched the coat.

Half an hour later, convinced that honesty was the best policy and carrying the coat in a smart new bag, Elsie left the department store and was making her way home. She felt as though she was living in a dream or a film as she mulled over Bob's apparent indifference to the morning's little episode. It helped that his father owned the place. Over drinks in a smart office, to their mutual amazement, they learned that they lived only two stations apart on the Dartford loop line. Neighbours!

'Are you doing anything tonight?' Bob had asked as casually as he could. When she replied that she was not, his face had creased into the most wonderful smile. A fast worker, definitely Errol Flynn with just a hint of Clark Gable? Shirley, her closest girlfriend, would surely understand and forgive her non-attendance at the King's Head.

'Do you like Clark Gable?' Bob had enquired, 'because I do, and *Gone with the Wind* is on again at the Regal in Sidcup. I've seen it twice already but...'

'So have I, Bob!' They had laughed.

Standing on the concourse of Charing Cross station, thinking about the highs and lows of an eventful day, Elsie smiled to herself when she recalled his reaction to her concern and remorse over the "theft" of a lovely maroon coat.

'Frankly, my dear,' he had said, holding her lightly by the waist, 'I don't give a damn!'

ON SAFARI

By Janet Winson

The cocktail hour was in full swing, the sound of quiet but lively chatter occasionally interrupted by the noise of the crusher in the ice machine at the back of the bar.

The hotel terrace at the Ya Ya Safari resort overlooked the wide plains of the Maasai Mara, a 60- minute flight in a small light aircraft from Nairobi Airport. In the air-conditioned reception area, which led onto the bar terrace, colourful flowering plants adorned the spaces between the chairs and tables. One side of the terrace was protected by a high crystal-clear Perspex screen. Guests who chose to stay late in the evening sometimes got a glimpse of grazing hippopotami quite close to the boundary of the terrace screen.

Dorothy Butters, a new arrival that afternoon, and her husband, George, were celebrating their 40th wedding anniversary; the safari was a gift from their four children. Dorothy had been excited about this trip for the best part of a year but now felt nervous, having seen the overnight accommodation, which was a large luxury tent with a huge mosquito net over the king-sized double bed. She fretted, doubting that the unknown and raw nature all around her could truly sit comfortably alongside the sheer luxury of the place. George patted her hand and ordered her another gin and tonic. Sure enough, she began to feel more relaxed as the alcohol hit the right spot in her weary traveller's brain.

The half-Kenyan Badejo family, a father with three growing children, looked relaxed even on soft drinks; the owner of the Ya Ya was the father's brother, Mal, and the children had been regular visitors over the years, coming on alternate summers when not staying over with their maternal Italian grandparents near Lake Como.

Dorothy recognised the family from the second flight to the resort and remembered seeing them in the departure lounge at Heathrow when they had joined the queue for first class passengers. The youngsters had a relaxed and confident air about them; there were twin girls of about 15 and a younger brother who seemed to be the clown of the family. The girls were looking immaculate in their designer travel wear, which was still fresh and un-creased. Dorothy glanced down at her rumpled cotton skirt and then at the small but obvious stain on her white sleeveless blouse, and she grabbed her bag, putting it on her lap to hide the stain. She was beginning to feel slightly intimidated by the surroundings. All the other guests on the terrace looked like they had been staying there for a while and knew the ropes. She decided it must be time for bed.

George and Dorothy found their way back to the tented area. Darkness had fallen swiftly and covered them like a blanket, but they had been given a powerful torch, which they used to guide them through the fragrant gardens until they reached their own tent. The bed had been turned back for them and covered in rose petals; a dim hurricane lamp was lit by the bed. Dorothy struggled to lay out their clean clothes for the morning, which was safari day number one. Though soothed by the drinks her anxiety remained, but, with the thought of an extra-early start and through sheer exhaustion, she was soon engulfed in slumber.

Dorothy and George were back on the terrace by 6.00 a.m. the following morning. Breakfast was laid out as a buffet and the delicious smell of Kenyan coffee beans and warm fresh rolls and croissants made them both feel hungry. Leaving their tent, they had marvelled at the loudness of the dawn chorus and were amazed by the huge colourful butterflies as they strolled out through the beautiful hotel gardens, full of fragrant frangipani. The couple, dressed similarly in long linen shorts, cotton shirts and Panama hats, were ready for a fantastic day complete with lunch en-route, a day with everything provided for them.

There was obviously some sort of problem at the reception desk as they walked past. Makena, the pleasant and smiling receptionist from the day before, was looking harassed and speaking very loudly on the telephone. Around her were six or seven angry-looking hotel guests talking loudly amongst themselves and failing to stay either polite or calm. Dorothy asked one of the English-speaking waiters what had happened. He said that the safe keys had gone missing overnight and the guests that were complaining had all left expensive cameras in the safe and were now panicking that they would not have them for the safari, which would make the whole day out pointless for them.

Dorothy was glad that her own digital camera was in her shoulder bag and she and George sat down to eat as far away as they could from the incident and resultant noise in reception. The owner, Mal Badejo, hurried past them after a few minutes. He greeted them with "Jumba" (hello) but at the same time, Dorothy suspected that he was in bad temper.

Two shiny new Jeeps drove up to the front of the hotel, chauffeured by Kamante and Joseph, Maasai warriors from the local tribe who lived in a village nearby. The men were both very tall, slim and dressed in traditional red robes. George was introduced to them and said they gave a really authentic feel to the excursion. They were the usual drivers for the safari trips and were well-trained guides with very good English, both clearly charming hosts and part of the hotel staff despite not living in.

The other guests were now arriving to join the safari, having been back to their tents to find or borrow spare cameras. They said they had all been offered money off the trip as compensation for the trouble with the safe. Makena had assured them that the safe would be forced open, if necessary, by tonight. The two guides were posing by the vehicles, their bangled arms around the shoulders of the guests; those with cameras were snapping away and taking selfies.

The guests were divided into two parties and George and Dorothy found themselves with the Badejo children, who explained that their father was staying behind to give his brother Mal a hand with sorting out the mystery of the lost keys. He had been on many safaris over the years and trusted the guides to look after his three children for the day. The young boy, Issa, was being comforted by his twin sisters as he loudly objected to sharing a camera with them. The problem with the safe threatened to have the potential to spoil the day for some of the guests. However, when the drivers started the engines and pulled away, all the upset seemed to dissolve, and excitement and expectation took over. The journey began with binoculars and cameras at the ready and the Mara lay ahead below the enormous Kenyan sky: wide, red-tinged and breath-taking.

The drivers had rigged up their intercom and microphones and stopped quite suddenly as two graceful giraffes suddenly appeared on the far horizon. It was the first of many photo opportunities.

George and Dorothy's driver was Kamante; he had the lead vehicle and was soon fully explaining the terrain and the variety of wildlife they expected to see during the day. He had a well-supplied cold bag in the boot, full of soft drinks and Tusker, the local beer, for the adults. The five passengers were soon relaxed and Dorothy found she was beginning to like the Badejo children. The girls, Mary and Faith, took photos of George and Dorothy in the Jeep with Dorothy's camera. They were fascinated that the couple had been married for so long; Mary said it was "totally amazing". They confided that their parents were divorced but the pay-off was the fabulous summer holidays every year, each parent keen to out-do the other. Issa, their ten-year-old brother, swapped seats to chat with George, who told him about his own similarly-aged grandson, Alfie, back home in Richmond-upon-Thames. It was beginning to feel like a family party.

Lunch was a planned stop for 1.00 p.m.at a pre-arranged destination. At about 12.15 p.m. Kamante assured them that they were at a completely safe area near the National Park and they all left the vehicle to stand by a river, where enormous hippopotami were basking, then hiding under the water and re-appearing snorting and blowing bubbles. It was so entertaining nobody wanted to leave, but time was limited, and everyone bundled back into the vehicle after 20 minutes. Dorothy was relieved; she had put on a good face but hated leaving the vehicle and had resorted to one of her anxiety pills.

They were about to set off again for lunch when Kamante received a message via the intercom; there seemed to be a lot of interference and the conversation was in some sort of dialect. Dorothy and George both sensed a difficulty. Kamante, no longer smiling, said their vehicle possibly had a fault and they might have to turn back early. He stopped the vehicle and waved down the following jeep. Suddenly he and Joseph, who had left his own vehicle, were huddled in a spot under some wide, shady trees in deep conversation, far enough away to not be overheard.

"Joseph, take the alternative route back to the Ya Ya. Follow me for a short while and then disappear. The big boss in Mombasa has been arrested and they're after me now. I think Mal's brother has talked him into confessing what's been going on. He'll soon be sorry and so will his boyfriend, Taivo. Keep the tourists calm though, Joseph. Stick to the story about the problems with the engine."

Both drivers returned within a few minutes and, after profuse apologies to the passengers, they started off again but this time much faster than before. When they passed a family group of elephants feeding just a way off there were no photo opportunities and the journey became faster and very rough.

Dorothy could not identify any particular reason for it but she had a sinking feeling in her gut and was shaking despite the intense heat of the midday sun. The twins, seeing that she looked upset, had moved to sit either side of her and they tried singing to cheer her up, but in her unease she remained quiet. Meanwhile, George still had his arm around Issa after realising that the little boy was crying silently. George coaxed him to share his very worst worries and was alarmed by what Issa said.

"Uncle Mal and Dad were talking last night. They thought I was listening to music with my ear pods but I heard every word. There's real trouble back at the Ya Ya. Money and passports have been stolen from the safe. Uncle Mal was talking about firing Kamante and his girlfriend, Makena but I think he is too scared of Kamante to do it. Kamante has another job down in Mombasa when there are no tourists for safari. Most of his friends are down on the beach there. The other thing is that Uncle Mal has been so sad since Taivo left the Ya Ya. He can't find another chef anywhere; he and Taivo were special best buddies. Something isn't right, George. How come the Jeep has engine problems when Kamante is driving it so fast now? I just want my dad."

Issa was distraught, crying and hiccupping, and George was afraid he was going to be sick. This drive was frightening enough for the grown-ups; the vehicle bumped over rough terrain at a ridiculous speed and almost lost balance a few times as Kamante recklessly took the corners. George tried to imagine whatever could be going on back at the Ya Ya – he remembered Mal's angry face that morning and acknowledged to himself that Kamante had shown a smug and superior air of confidence, masked by his great bonhomie. It was obvious that Issa was a very smart 10-year-old and George began to think that what he had said was certainly possible, even likely.

George looked back to see how the other Jeep was keeping up and was very shocked to realise it was no longer there. He shouted out to Kamante, who didn't turn his head or answer.

Issa whispered to George, "At bedtime last night Dad said this could well be our last holiday at the Ya Ya."

Fifteen minutes later, a loud vehicle could be heard behind them. George turned his head expecting to see Joseph driving the second Jeep at speed but instead was astonished to see a large, black pick-up truck with no markings tearing along the Mara and gaining on them, eventually tail-gating them. George was still trying to make sense of it all when he heard a couple of rifle shots and there was a sudden sharp pain in his left arm. He pushed Issa's head down and shouted to Dorothy and the twins, "Get down, get down! Someone is shooting at us!"

Before he blacked out, George caught a glimpse of Dorothy's look of terror and disbelief; it was a look that would become ingrained in his mind

*

George was coming around slowly; he realised he was lying on the ground and he could feel blood running down his arm. The Jeep was on its side and he could see nobody around until his eyes scanned the immediate area and he finally saw Dorothy lying in a foetal position beside the Jeep; she was shaking and crying. There was no sign of the Badejo children.

"Dorothy, are you hurt? What happened, where's our driver? Whatever happened to the Jeep? Where have the children gone?"

In a small, shaky voice she replied: "The pick-up truck jammed into us, side on, and the jeep crashed. There was a gang of men in masks carrying guns and rifles. They beat up Kamante and marched him off somewhere. Then they rounded up the kids and put them into the truck and drove away with them. Before they left, they pulled both you and me out of the back of the Jeep. I think they thought we were both dead. I was awake but acted dumb and kept still. I really thought you were dead though, George. You were unconscious for a good while."

The long speech had taken Dorothy's last vestige of energy and they decided to hide out in the shelter of the wrecked Jeep, silently praying for safety. Dorothy found her husband's large handkerchief and made a makeshift pad as a covering for George's arm, which had stopped bleeding by now.

*

Young Alfie Butters, watching TV with his parents, was upset to see his grandparents on Sky News the next day; they were both in hospital. Speculation continued about the attack as the Badejo children, who at first were thought to have been kidnapped, had been taken back to the Ya Ya much later on, very scared but unharmed. Kamante's body was found the same afternoon with a bullet in his brain; he had been wanted for his part in a huge drug smuggling operation in Mombasa for some time. Tourists generally were unaware of the serious hub of world drug trafficking that is rife in Kenya. At first Mal Badejo, owner of the Ya Ya, was suspected of being involved in the incident but when his nieces and nephews were delivered safely back to the hotel that evening, the investigation took a different turn.

When George and Dorothy were back at Heathrow they were met by a huge gaggle of reporters. The popular tabloids headlined: 'Massacre after breakfast. Surrey pensioners return safely after their special anniversary holiday.'

The story was dropped within a few days and George and Dorothy were famous in their home town for about a fortnight. They didn't fly again during their remaining years.

The Badejo children were soon back home with their mother; their father's words were indeed proven true as the events had hastened their final trip to Kenya.

Mal Badejo was charged with hiring a perpetrator for the murder of Kamante, who had been blackmailing him; other members of the hotel staff as well as Kamante knew all about Mal's long-term partner, the award-winning chef at the Ya Ya, and that if someone exposed them, he could serve a maximum of 16 years under Section 162 of the penal code. Homosexuality was still outlawed in Kenya and a common reason for many blackmail offences. The blackmail money taken from Mal had helped fund the massive drug racket that Kamante had been running for years. Now, Mal was himself exposed as a broken man, his business ruined.

He was never to return to the Ya Ya as nobody would ever risk taking it on in future now its reputation was thoroughly ruined. The Ya Ya resort was pulled down and nowadays the hippopotami have a little more grazing space.

THAT'S MY GLOVE

By Jan Brown

"You want a deal on that thing?"

His name badge identified him as 'Troy' and his huge head bobbed about on his insubstantial stick neck as he leaned over and nudged his colleague in the ribs. "What can we give him for that, Ky?"

'Ky' snorted, "Don't call me Ky." She stood up, simultaneously yawning and stretching, before reaching over for a large, pink bowl-shaped mug inscribed *'Kylie hearts Kevin'* and slinking away. "You want a coffee, Troy boy?"

It seemed I didn't warrant a coffee.

"So…what sort of car are you looking for?" Troy poked a grubby fingernail into the gappy bits of his teeth and examined the resulting debris carefully before flicking it away.

"Something a bit faster. Definitely a bigger boot." I pointed up at the Ford Tourneo poster. "That sort of thing would be amazing."

"It would indeed be amazing, mate."

I did not, and would not, ever consider us to be mates.

Again, the head bobbed, as if enjoying its own private joke. "More amazing to me would be how you think you're gonna pay for a half decent motor."

I had considered offering the Datsun Sunny in part exchange before Troy stamped on my thought, killing it.

"Because you won't get anywhere with that thing. Now get it off our forecourt. Clear off with your old tat. You'll give us a bad name."

I kept a magnificently cool head – dead Uncle Terry would surely have been proud of that – and left in a calm and composed manner.

*

The next morning, I felt strangely cheerful. I got up, which is always a good start, and opened the curtains, squinting in shock at the onslaught of light. I then mooched around my flat, humming vaguely familiar tunes, and nodded happily. I liked this flat, my sanctuary, and for once it wasn't too messy. 'Homely', I would describe it.

I looked in the fridge and a bit of gloom descended; absolutely nothing in there that could be described as edible. A mouldy red pepper looked me in the eye, almost sulkily, aggrieved that I had kept it captive for so long, festering and alone. The only other occupant was the crumbling remains of a blueberry cheesecake; that and the red pepper were not good fridge-fellows, which was why I had stored them on separate shelves in the first place. I had briefly considered eating the cheesecake but the blueberries had shrivelled and the so-called cheese part was pulsating and green.

So, there was nothing to eat, and I was hungry; I'd had a very late, very productive night out and really felt I deserved some milk and muffins to satisfy my hunger.

A pint of milk and a muffin, that was all I had wanted last night, but then I couldn't find my other black glove and that's when it all started to go wrong. Agitated, I remembered my Uncle Terry again. "You'd forget your head if it wasn't screwed on, Ronnie," he would jeer at me, a relentless undercurrent against the Saturday afternoon football scores. Ronnie nil – Uncle Terry scores again.

But I'm getting ahead of myself. In fact, that's something else my long departed 'uncle' loved to throw at me. "You're ahead of your time, Ronnie," he would say gleefully, clacking his lower set of teeth at me, which I always found quite repulsive, having successfully managed to retain all of my own teeth. I quite liked the accolade 'ahead of your time' though. Ironic, I think you'd say.

I referred to him as 'uncle' but always harboured a suspicion that Terry was something of a trophy hunter, with the prize being my rather glamorous mother – how she had loved to drape herself all over him. When she began the familiar process of peeling off her long black silk gloves, one red-tipped finger at a time, in slow languorous movements, I would stare greedily, mouth agape, until a well-aimed blow from Terry would send me spinning.

I had left my flat quickly, keen to avoid conversation with those individuals who liked to talk for the sake of it, for the pure joy of opening one's mouth and just spouting out any nonsense that happened to be waiting to be released, just behind the frontal lobe.

It then occurred to me that in my rush I hadn't bothered with a shower. If I had realised I was going to be apprehended by the police, I would of course have followed the traditional behaviour pattern that many people seem to stick to, but I didn't. Look down on me for that if you must but, let's face it, who hasn't neglected the social niceties and nipped out for a muffin? I'd opted for a quick whizz round with my deodorant stick, and actually, on reflection, probably overdid the 'Frescia Freshness' somewhat, judging by the way the police officer had screwed up his nose.

Anyway, I was more concerned that I couldn't find my glove. Its right-handed partner was in my jacket pocket but the left hander, the main protagonist, I call it, was nowhere to be seen. I hoped it was in the car and hadn't dropped out somewhere, lying abandoned in a gutter. I had worn the gloves at Mother's funeral, holding her perfect face in my black silk-clad fingers for one last time. The funeral director had been very patient as I'd rearranged her head on the pillow, fluffing her hair out onto the silk pillowcase.

Quietly descending the stairs, I had made it to the communal entrance just as the door of the ground floor flat opened and Hetty Heggerty (ridiculous name for a ridiculous woman) peered out at me, her eyes naked and seemingly blind without the security of her glasses.

"Who's that?" she said. I didn't answer but just stood there, briefly savouring the buzz. "If that's you, Ronald, speak up. I'm looking for my Willy. Have you seen him?"

I had slammed the door behind me, careless as to the whereabouts of her aged tom-cat as long as he wasn't sitting on my Sunny.

"You want a deal on that thing?" Nope, it still hurt. The casual throwaway sarcasm astounded me; you don't treat a car like that. That car could tell some stories – if cars could speak, of course, and I realise none of them can.

It was the biggest motor I had ever owned and I loved the feeling of power as other lesser vehicles moved out of its way. It was old now, and battered, its original orange colour dulled and dusty. I had occasionally thought of trading up to maybe a Jeep or Land Rover, something a bit more practical, but my one and only visit to a car showroom had been met with mocking hilarity. I knew it had been a mistake even as I began the seemingly endless journey through the vast open showroom space to the reception desk situated in a far corner – something I later mentioned to my solicitor.

I didn't feel I needed a solicitor but you know how they wear you down. I admit I did lead them on a bit of a chase, but I hadn't realised the exhaust was hanging off my car and I should have checked the boot was locked; big mistake, that.

"You want a deal on that thing?" repeated over and over in my head.

I still wanted milk for my coffee and muffins, or a single muffin, but you couldn't always buy them individually. If forced, I would have purchased the four pack and eaten one a day. The requirement for milk was annoying as I hated the smell of it, the sour sickly stink of the little school bottles from the 70s – not cold and not even hot, but just warm and rank. I felt bile rising momentarily, as if the memory of warm milk was a smell itself.

The roads had been fairly quiet as I mused on, slowing as a potential shop came in sight but not stopping. I hadn't given Sunny a proper run out for a while so I put my foot down. "Let's see if you've still got it, girl."

I enjoyed the green blur as I rushed past trees and small blurry humans, which were little more than momentary blobs of colour. I don't know how long the police car had been following me, but I became aware of it discretely shadowing me before flashing me to stop; then, as I sped up again, headlights blinking angrily and siren blaring. Sunny was doing her best, but she was old and feeble, like an aged parent. It was the peculiar, whining shriek seemingly emitting from her soul that had finally convinced me to stop; goodness knows what damage I'd done to her.

"Do you know why I stopped you, sir?" He leaned in through the open window, forcing me into unappealingly close contact with his ginger beard.

"Er, I would say maybe I was going just a bit too fast."

PC Ginger Beard bizarrely chuckled, revealing grey, tombstone teeth. "You weren't going that fast, sir, not in this beauty, but you were making a terrible noise. Perhaps we could have a little chat about your exhaust?" He had gestured me towards Sunny's rear.

"Are you a fan of the Datsun Sunny, officer?" I'd picked up on his use of the word 'beauty'.

"They're great cars. I used to have a similar model in my younger days. You wouldn't believe the things I got up to." He slapped affectionately at Sunny's boot and that part of her sprang open joyously, inviting inspection.

He peered in, engulfed by the emerging smell. "Oh my god almighty, what have you done?" He staggered away, clutching onto Sunny's wing mirror.

Nestling in the boot, the long black silk fingers of the glove pointed elegantly at Troy's head, his reddened eyes looking on sightlessly.

"That's my glove." I smiled triumphantly at the officer. Mother would have been pleased.

THE THEFT

By Glynne Covell

There's been an incident,
a burglary in fact.
It's left me feeling quite bereft
to be the victim of such an act.
Someone's stolen my zest, my bounce,
they've taken it away!
A very nasty deed it was
and it's left my hair quite grey.
The robber also stole my legs,
have you ever heard of such a thing?
Left me with someone else's pegs,
and wrinkles when I grin.
Oh, it's so upsetting to have such shock
it's a very personal blow
to be robbed in daylight of my youth
has left me feeling low.
But, let me think again on this,
maybe I should not lament.
I'm safely out to pasture now
to just be me…content!

ABOUT THE AUTHORS

The TEN GREEN JOTTERS of Sidcup:

C.G Harris

C. G Harris hails from Kent, England, UK. He is a former winner of the *William Van Wert Award* for a fiction short story. His book *Light and Dark: 21 Short Stories* was shortlisted for the *"Words for the Wounded" Independent Author Award* and has received critical acclaim. His second collection, *Kisses from the Sun and Other Stories* was released in June 2020 to similar praise. He is currently working on a series of detective short stories.

He has a wife, two daughters, three grandchildren, one dog and a cat. He plays the guitar, ukulele and juggles...although not necessarily all at the same time.

Jan Brown

Jan Brown, aka Emily the Writer, has always loved writing, ambitiously penning her own Starsky & Hutch story at the age of 12, although she never actually allowed anyone else to read it.

Jan has had a number of articles, interviews and short stories published and is a prize winner in, and regular contributor to, The Monthly Seagull magazine and to the Charlton Athletic fanzine. She lives with her partner and loves anything furry with four legs.

Glynne Covell

Glynne's "Carpe Diem" attitude to life has found her trekking in New Guinea and the foothills of the Himalayas', hot air ballooning and, closer to home, climbing Big Ben and the O2. London born; she is yet descended from the French Huguenots.

Married, with two children, and grandchildren, her hobbies of travelling, history and calligraphy all have links with her writing for which she has a very special passion (this, and chocolate!). She is delighted to be able to contribute to this, the second anthology by the Ten Green Jotters of Sidcup.

Julia Gale

Originally from Carlisle, then brought up in Southampton, Julia moved to London in 1995 after marrying her husband, Colin. Julia was a prodigious early reader as a child. Always with a book in her hand this may well have fuelled her desire to become an author, and she began by writing poems for the local church magazine. Over the years she has had a variety of jobs but since being married has been a full-time mother and house wife, occasionally finding time to do voluntary work; with Colin, she has two grown up daughters and a disabled son. Her hobbies are cooking and gardening.

Her observations on people, the real-life situations they find themselves in and life's many ups and downs are reflected in her stories.

A.J.R. Kinchington

Edinburgh born she currently lives in London.

A writing competition win at eleven years old started her on a life-long love of story-telling.

Three children and a twenty-five-year career in psychotherapy gave little time to write for pleasure but a note-book to jot down ideas was always to hand.

Travel to many countries has been an inspiration and now retired she has time for the necessity to write. She hopes to complete her semi-biographical story of her Scottish great-grandparents.

Richard Miller

Richard has lived most of his life in Sidcup, birthplace of the Ten Green Jotters. Although much of his working career was spent in London as a Network and Telecommunications Manager in a Government Department, his job also required him to visit more exotic locations including Barbados, India, South Africa and Thailand. Switching from writing technical documents to penning something more creative has proved challenging but rewarding.

He is a season ticket holder at Chelsea FC (he has followed the club for more years than he cares to remember) and enjoys real ale, whisky, blues music and history. At home Richard has several hundred books and records plus over forty bottles of single malt whisky. He is a member of a number of historical societies.

Tony Ormerod

Derby born, and dreaming of journalism, at 16 Tony inexplicably rejected a job offer with the local *Evening Telegraph*. Employment in the warm bosom of Local Government beckoned and then, migrating way down South [Hove], he progressed to Bromley Council where he was later declared surplus to requirements. A career in financial services led to early retirement and an ambition to do nothing was achieved.

Occasionally, this idleness is interrupted by articles published in the aforementioned newspaper plus a couple more in the 'Best of British' magazine. After 52 years he remains married to the same lovely wife. She pleads anonymity.

Richie Stress

Richie has always liked words. He has used them to write short stories, scripts for television and award- winning poetry.

In 2008 he was talked into studying for a Creative Writing degree by a very enthusiastic lady from the Open University...and which he completed a mere seven years later. He also presents regular podcasts together with his partner where he is under strict instructions not to be crude or use bad language. His favourite animal is the snow leopard.

Janet Winson

Janet hopes that you enjoy her two stories within this collection; both inspired by actual events held in her memory. Story telling always ran in her family and was fuelled by a colourful 60's childhood in South London. It has been a long process but following some short courses and a few years as part of a local writing group the stories started to come.

The value of good fiction was never greater than in Janet's 40's when she was suddenly widowed with two children at home and reading became an elixir and an escape; it still remains as such. Retirement brought with it the luxury of time and the stories began to flow; stories of real people, real places and life-changing events are of greatest interest to her.

Swimming and gardening also remain major pleasures. Janet happily re-married just pre-retirement. She has one daughter, two sons and two grandchildren plus three grand-dogs!

Lily the Dog

Lily is the honorary member and mascot of the group. She is seven years old, a springer spaniel, and her interests consist of eating, "squirrel-chasing" by day and "fox-watching" in the evening. She was inspired to join the group after reading that Timmy the dog was a founder member of the Famous Five.

She has not displayed any literary talent as yet but the remainder of the group remain optimistic.